EX LIBRIS

NAME

THE SLIPPERY SLOPE

✳ A Series of Unfortunate Events ✳

BOOK the Tenth

THE SLIPPERY SLOPE

by LEMONY SNICKET

Illustrations by Brett Helquist

⬛ HARPERCOLLINS*Publishers*

Library of Congress Cataloging-in-Publication Data
Snicket, Lemony.
  The slippery slope / by Lemony Snicket ; illustrations by Brett Helquist.
    p. cm. — (A series of unfortunate events ; bk. the 10th)
  Summary: In the perilous Mortmain Mountains, Klaus and Violet
Baudelaire meet another well-read person, who helps them try to rescue
Sunny from the villainous Count Olaf and his henchmen as they all near "the
last safe place."
  ISBN 978-0-06-441013-7 — ISBN 978-0-06-029641-4 (lib. bdg.)
ISBN 978-0-06-286512-0 (special edition)
  [1. Orphans—Fiction. 2. Brothers and sisters—Fiction.
3. Mountains—Fiction. 4. Humorous stories.] I. Helquist, Brett, ill. II. Title.
PZ7.S6795 Si 2003   2003013267
[Fic]—dc22   CIP
                                                               AC

      18 19 20 21 22   PC/LSCH   60 59 58 57 56 55 54 53
                                   ❖
                          First Edition, 2003
        Visit us on the World Wide Web! www.harpercollinschildrens.com

❊

For Beatrice—
When we met, you were pretty, and I was lonely.
Now, I am pretty lonely.

CHAPTER One

A man of my acquaintance once wrote a poem called "The Road Less Traveled," describing a journey he took through the woods along a path most travelers never used. The poet found that the road less traveled was peaceful but quite lonely, and he was probably a bit nervous as he went along, because if anything happened on the road less traveled, the other travelers would be on the road more frequently traveled and so couldn't hear him as he cried for help. Sure enough, that poet is now dead.

Like a dead poet, this book can be said to be on the road less traveled, because it begins with the three Baudelaire children on a path

leading through the Mortmain Mountains, which
is not a popular destination for travelers, and it
ends in the churning waters of the Stricken
Stream, which few travelers even go near. But
this book is also on the road less traveled,
because unlike books most people prefer, which
provide comforting and entertaining tales about
charming people and talking animals, the tale
you are reading now is nothing but distressing
and unnerving, and the people unfortunate
enough to be in the story are far more desperate and frantic than charming, and I would prefer to not speak about the animals at all. For that
reason, I can no more suggest the reading of this
woeful book than I can recommend wandering
around the woods by yourself, because like the
road less traveled, this book is likely to make
you feel lonely, miserable, and in need of help.

The Baudelaire orphans, however, had no
choice but to be on the road less traveled. Violet and Klaus, the two elder Baudelaires, were
in a caravan, traveling very quickly along the

high mountain path. Neither Violet, who was fourteen, nor Klaus, who had recently turned thirteen, had ever thought they would find themselves on this road, except perhaps with their parents on a family vacation. But the Baudelaire parents were nowhere to be found after a terrible fire destroyed their home— although the children had reason to believe that one parent may not have died in the blaze after all—and the caravan was not heading up the Mortmain Mountains, toward a secret headquarters the siblings had heard about and were hoping to find. The caravan was heading down the Mortmain Mountains, very quickly, with no way to control or stop its journey, so Violet and Klaus felt more like fish in a stormy sea than travelers on a vacation.

But Sunny Baudelaire was in a situation that could be said to be even more desperate. Sunny was the youngest Baudelaire, still learning to speak in a way that everyone could understand, so she scarcely had words for how frightened she was. Sunny was traveling uphill, toward the headquarters in the Mortmain Mountains, in an automobile that was working perfectly, but the driver of the automobile was a man who was reason enough for being terrified. Some people called this man wicked. Some called him faci-norous, which is a fancy word for "wicked." But everyone called him Count Olaf, unless he was wearing one of his ridiculous disguises and making people call him a false name. Count Olaf was an actor, but he had largely abandoned his theatrical career to try to steal the enormous fortune the Baudelaire parents had left behind. Olaf's schemes to get the fortune had been mean-spirited and particularly complicated, but nevertheless he had managed to attract a girl-friend, a villainous and stylish woman named Esmé Squalor, who was sitting next to Count Olaf in the car, cackling nastily and clutching Sunny on her lap. Also in the car were several employees of Olaf's, including a man with hooks instead of hands, two women who liked to wear white powder all over their faces, and three new comrades Olaf had recently recruited at Caligari Carnival. The Baudelaire children had been at the carnival, too, wearing disguises of their own, and had pretended to join Count Olaf in his treachery, but the villain had seen through their ruse, a phrase which here means "realized who they really were, and cut the knot attaching the caravan to the car, leaving Sunny in Olaf's clutches and her siblings tumbling toward their doom." Sunny sat in the car and felt Esmé's long fingernails scratch her shoulders, and worried about what would happen to her and what was happening to her older siblings, as she heard their screams getting fainter and fainter as the car drove farther and farther away.

"We have to stop this caravan!" Klaus screamed. Hurriedly, he put on his glasses, as if by improving his vision he might improve the situation. But even in perfect focus, he could see their predicament was dire. The caravan had served as a home for several performers at the carnival's House of Freaks before they defected—a word which here means "joined Count Olaf's band of revolting comrades"—and now the contents of this tiny home were rattling and crashing with each bump in the road. Klaus ducked to avoid a roasting pan, which Hugo the hunchback had used to prepare meals and which had toppled off a shelf in the commotion. He lifted his feet from the floor as a set of dominoes skittered by—a set that Colette the contortionist had liked to play with. And he squinted above him as a hammock swung violently overhead. An ambidextrous person named Kevin used to sleep in that hammock until he had joined Olaf's troupe, along with Hugo and Colette, and now it seemed like it might fall at any moment and trap the Baudelaires beneath it.

The only comforting thing that Klaus could see was his sister, who was looking around the caravan with a fierce and thoughtful expression and unbuttoning the shirt the two siblings were sharing as part of their disguise. "Help me get us out of these freakish pants we're both in," Violet said. "There's no use pretending we're a two-headed person anymore, and we both need to be as able-bodied as possible."

In moments, the two Baudelaires wriggled out of the oversized clothing they had taken from Count Olaf's disguise kit and were standing in regular clothes, trying to balance in the shaky caravan. Klaus quickly stepped out of the path of a falling potted plant, but he couldn't help smiling as he looked at his sister. Violet was tying her hair up in a ribbon to keep it out of her eyes, a sure sign that she was thinking up an invention. Violet's impressive mechanical skills had saved the Baudelaires' lives more times than they could count, and Klaus was certain that his sister could concoct something that could stop the caravan's perilous journey.

"Are you going to make a brake?" Klaus asked.

"Not yet," Violet said. "A brake interferes with the wheels of a vehicle, and this caravan's wheels are spinning too quickly for interference. I'm going to unhook these hammocks and use them as a drag chute."

"Drag chute?" Klaus said.

"Drag chutes are a little like parachutes attached to the back of a car," Violet explained hurriedly, as a coatrack clattered around her. She reached up to the hammock where she and Klaus had slept and quickly detached it from the wall. "Race drivers use them to help stop their cars when a race is over. If I dangle these hammocks out the caravan door, we should slow down considerably."

"What can I do?" Klaus said.

"Look in Hugo's pantry," Violet said, "and see if you can find anything sticky."

When someone tells you to do something unusual without an explanation, it is very difficult not to ask why, but Klaus had learned long ago to have faith in his sister's ideas, and quickly crossed to a large cupboard Hugo had used to store ingredients for the meals he prepared. The door of the cupboard was swinging back and forth as if a ghost were fighting with it, but most of the items were still rattling around inside. Klaus looked at the cupboard and thought of his baby sister, who was getting farther and farther away from him. Even though Sunny was still quite young, she had recently shown an interest in cooking, and Klaus remembered how she had made up her own hot chocolate recipe, and helped prepare a delicious soup the entire caravan had enjoyed. Klaus held the cupboard door open and peered inside, and hoped that his sister would survive to develop her culinary skills.

"*Klaus,*" Violet said firmly, taking down another hammock and tying it to the first one. "I don't mean to rush you, but we need to stop this caravan as soon as possible. Have you found anything sticky?"

Klaus blinked and returned to the task at

hand. A ceramic pitcher rolled around his feet as he pushed through the bottles and jars of cooking materials. "There's lots of sticky things here," he said. "I see blackstrap molasses, wild clover honey, corn syrup, aged balsamic vinegar, apple butter, strawberry jam, caramel sauce, maple syrup, butterscotch topping, maraschino liqueur, virgin and extra-virgin olive oil, lemon curd, dried apricots, mango chutney, *crema di noci*, tamarind paste, hot mustard, marshmallows, creamed corn, peanut butter, grape preserves, salt water taffy, condensed milk, pumpkin pie filling, and glue. I don't know why Hugo kept glue in the pantry, but never mind. Which items do you want?"

"All of them," Violet said firmly. "Find some way of mixing them, while I tie these hammocks together."

Klaus grabbed the pitcher from the floor and began to pour the ingredients into it, while Violet, sitting on the floor to make it easier to balance, gathered the cords of the hammocks in her lap and began twisting them into a knot. The caravan's journey grew rougher and rougher, and with each jolt, the Baudelaires felt a bit seasick, as if they were back on Lake Lachrymose, crossing its stormy waters to try and rescue one of their many unfortunate guardians. But despite the tumult around them, in moments Violet stood up with the hammocks gathered in her arms, all tied together in a mass of fabric, and Klaus looked at his sister and held up the pitcher, which was filled to the brim with a thick and colorful slime.

"When I say the word," Violet said, "I'm going to open the door and cast these hammocks out. I want you at the other end of the caravan, Klaus. Open that little window and pour that mixture all over the wheels. If the hammocks work as a drag chute and the sticky substance interferes with the wheels, the caravan should slow down enough to save us. I just need to tie the hammocks to the doorknob."

"Are you using the Devil's Tongue knot?" Klaus asked.

"The Devil's Tongue hasn't brought us the best luck," Violet said, referring to several previous rope-related escapades. "I'm using the Sumac, a knot I invented myself. I named it after a singer I admire. There—it feels secure. Are you ready to pour that mixture onto the wheels?"

Klaus crossed to the window and opened it. The wild clattering sound of the caravan's wheels grew louder, and the Baudelaires stared for a moment at the countryside racing by. The land was jagged and twisty, and it seemed that the caravan could tumble at any moment into a hole, or off the edge of one of the mountain's square peaks. "I guess I'm ready," Klaus said hesitantly. "Violet, before we try your invention, I want to tell you something."

"If we don't try it now," Violet said grimly, "you won't have the chance to tell me anything." She gave her knot one more tug and then turned back to Klaus. "Now!" she said, and threw open the caravan door.

It is often said that if you have a room with a view, you will feel peaceful and relaxed, but if the room is a caravan hurtling down a steep and twisted road, and the view is an eerie mountain range racing backward away from you, while chilly mountain winds sting your face and toss dust into your eyes, then you will not feel one bit of peace or relaxation. Instead you will feel the horror and panic that the Baudelaires felt when Violet opened the door. For a moment they could do nothing but stand still, feeling the wild tilting of the caravan, and looking up at the odd, square peaks of the Mortmain Mountains, and hearing the grinding of the caravan's wheels as they rolled over rocks and tree stumps. But then Violet shouted "Now!" once more, and both siblings snapped into action. Klaus leaned out the window and began to pour the mixture of blackstrap molasses, wild clover honey, corn syrup, aged balsamic vinegar, apple butter, strawberry jam, caramel sauce, maple syrup, butterscotch topping, maraschino liqueur, virgin and extra-virgin olive oil, lemon curd, dried apricots, mango chutney, *crema di noci*, tamarind paste, hot mustard, marshmallows, creamed corn, peanut butter, grape preserves, salt water taffy, condensed milk, pumpkin pie filling, and glue onto the closest wheels, while his sister tossed the hammocks out of the door, and if you have read anything of the Baudelaire orphans' lives—which I hope you have not—then you will not be surprised to read that Violet's invention worked perfectly. The hammocks immediately caught the rushing air and swelled out behind the caravan like enormous cloth balloons, which slowed the caravan down quite a bit, the way you would run much slower if you were dragging something behind you, like a knapsack or a sheriff. The sticky mixture fell on the spinning wheels, which immediately began to move with less ferocity, the way you would run with less ferocity if you suddenly found yourself running in quicksand or through lasagne. The caravan slowed down, and the wheels spun less wildly, and within moments the two Baudelaires were traveling at a much more comfortable pace.

"It's working!" Klaus cried.

"We're not done yet," Violet said, and walked over to a small table that had overturned in the confusion. When the Baudelaires were living at Caligari Carnival, the table had come in handy as a place to sit and make plans, but now in the Mortmain Mountains, it would come in handy for a different reason. Violet dragged the table over to the open door. "Now that the wheels are slowing down," she said, "we can use this as a brake."

Klaus dumped the last of the mixture out of the pitcher, and turned to his sister. "How?" he said, but Violet was already showing him how. Quickly she lay on the floor, and holding the table by its legs, dangled it out of the caravan so it dragged on the ground. Immediately there was a loud scraping sound, and the table began to shake roughly in Violet's hands. But she held fast, forcing the table to scrape against the rocky ground and slow the caravan down even more. The swaying of the caravan became gentler and gentler, and the fallen items owned by the carnival employees stopped crashing, and then with one last whine, the wheels stopped altogether, and everything was still. Violet leaned out of the door and stuck the table in front of one of the wheels so it couldn't start rolling again, and then stood up and looked at her brother.

"We did it," Violet said.

"*You* did it," Klaus said. "The entire plan was your idea." He put down the pitcher on the floor and wiped his hands on a fallen towel.

"Don't put down that pitcher," Violet said, looking around the wreckage of the caravan. "We should gather up as many useful things as possible. We'll need to get this caravan moving uphill if we want to rescue Sunny."

"And reach the headquarters," Klaus added.

"Count Olaf has the map we found, but I remember that the headquarters are in the Valley of Four Drafts, near the source of the Stricken Stream. It'll be very cold there."

"Well, there is plenty of clothing," Violet said, looking around. "Let's grab everything we can and organize it outside."

Klaus nodded in agreement, and picked up the pitcher again, along with several items of clothing that had fallen in a heap on top of a small hand mirror that belonged to Colette. Staggering from carrying so many things, he walked out of the caravan behind his sister, who was carrying a large bread knife, three heavy coats, and a ukulele that Hugo used to play sometimes on lazy afternoons. The floors of the caravan creaked as the Baudelaires stepped outside, into the misty and empty landscape, and realized how fortunate they had been.

The caravan had stopped right at the edge of one of the odd, square peaks of the mountain range. The Mortmain Mountains looked like a staircase, heading up into the clouds or down into a veil of thick, gray mist, and if the caravan had kept going in the same direction, the two Baudelaires would have toppled over the peak and fallen down through the mist to the next stair, far, far below. But to one side of the caravan, the children could see the waters of the Stricken Stream, which were an odd grayish black color, and moved slowly and lazily downhill like a river of spilled oil. Had the caravan swerved to one side, the children would have been dumped into the dark and filthy waters.

"It looks like the brake worked just in time," Violet said quietly. "No matter where the caravan would have gone, we would have been finished."

Klaus nodded in agreement and looked around at the wilderness. "It will be difficult to navigate the caravan out of here," Klaus said. "You'll have to invent a steering device."

"And some sort of engine," Violet said.

"That will take some time."

"We don't have any time," Klaus said. "If we don't hurry, Count Olaf will be too far away and we'll never find Sunny."

"We'll find her," Violet said firmly, and put down the items she was carrying. "Let's go back into the caravan, and look for—"

But before Violet could say what to look for, she was interrupted by an unpleasant crackling noise. The caravan seemed to moan, and then slowly began to roll toward the edge of the peak. The Baudelaires looked down and saw that the wheels had smashed the small table, so there was nothing to stop the caravan from moving again. Slowly and awkwardly it pitched forward, dragging the hammocks behind it as it neared the very edge of the peak. Klaus leaned down to grab hold of a hammock, but Violet stopped him. "It's too heavy," she said. "We can't stop it."

"We can't let it fall off the peak!" Klaus cried.

"We'd be dragged down, too," Violet said.

Klaus knew his sister was right, but still he wanted to grab the drag chute Violet had constructed. It is difficult, when faced with a situation you cannot control, to admit that you can do nothing, and it was difficult for the Baudelaires to stand and watch the caravan roll over the edge of the peak. There was one last creak as the back wheels bumped against a mound of dirt, and then the caravan disappeared in absolute silence. The Baudelaires stepped forward and peered over the edge of the peak, but it was so misty that the caravan was only a ghostly rectangle, getting smaller and smaller as it faded away.

"Why isn't there a crash?" Klaus asked.

"The drag chute is slowing it down," Violet said. "Just wait."

The siblings waited, and after a moment there was a muffled *boom!* from below as the caravan met its fate. In the mist, the children could not see a thing, but they knew that the caravan and everything inside it were gone forever, and indeed I have never been able to find its remains, even after months of searching the area with only a lantern and a rhyming dictionary for company. It seems that even after countless nights of battling snow gnats and praying the batteries would not run out, it is my fate that some of my questions will never be answered.

Fate is like a strange, unpopular restaurant, filled with odd waiters who bring you things you never asked for and don't always like. When the Baudelaires were very young, they would have guessed that their fate was to grow up in happiness and contentment with their parents in the Baudelaire mansion, but now both the mansion and their parents were gone. When they were attending Prufrock Preparatory School, they had thought that their fate was to graduate alongside their friends the Quagmires, but they hadn't seen the academy or the two triplets in a very long time. And just moments ago, it had looked like Violet and Klaus's fate had been to fall off a peak or into a stream, but now they were alive and well, but far away from their sister and without a vehicle to help them find her again.

Violet and Klaus moved closer to one another, and felt the icy winds of the Mortmain Mountains blow down the road less traveled and give them goosebumps. They looked at the dark and swirling waters of the Stricken Stream, and they looked down from the edge of the peak into the mist, and then looked at one another and shivered, not only at the fates they had avoided, but at all the mysterious fates that lay ahead.

CHAPTER TWO

Violet took one last look over the misty peak, and then reached down to put on one of the heavy coats she had taken from the caravan. "Take one of these coats," she said to her brother. "It's cold out here, and it's likely to get even colder. The headquarters are supposed to be very high up in the mountains. By the time we get there, we'll probably be wearing every stitch of this clothing."

"But how are we going to get there?" Klaus said. "We're nowhere near the Valley of Four Drafts, and the caravan is destroyed."

"Let's take a moment to see what we have,"

Violet said. "I might be able to construct something from the items we managed to take."

"I hope so," Klaus said. "Sunny is getting farther and farther away. We'll never catch up with her without some sort of vehicle."

Klaus spread out the items from the caravan, and put on one of the coats while Violet picked through her pile, but instantly the two Baudelaires saw that a vehicle was not in the realm of possibility, a phrase which here means "could not be made from a few small objects and some articles of clothing previously belonging to carnival employees." Violet tied her hair up in a ribbon again and frowned down on the few items they had managed to save. In Klaus's pile there was the pitcher, still sticky from the substance he had used to slow down the caravan wheels, as well as Colette's hand mirror, a wool poncho, and a sweatshirt that read CALIGARI CARNIVAL. In Violet's pile was the large bread knife, the ukulele, and one more coat. Even

Klaus, who was not as mechanically minded as his sister, knew that the materials gathered on the ground were not enough to make something that could take the two children through the Mortmain Mountains.

"I suppose I could make a spark by rubbing two rocks together," Violet said, looking around the misty countryside for additional inventing materials, "or we could play the ukulele and bang on the pitcher. A loud noise might attract some help."

"But who would hear it?" Klaus said, gazing at the gloomy mist. "We didn't see a sign of anyone else when we were in the caravan. The way through the Mortmain Mountains is like a poem I read once, about the road less traveled."

"Did the poem have a happy ending?" Violet asked.

"It was neither happy nor unhappy," Klaus said. "It was ambiguous. Well, let's gather up these materials and take them with us."

"Take them with us?" Violet said. "We don't know where to go, and we don't know how to get there."

"Sure we do," Klaus said. "The Stricken Stream starts at a source high in the mountains, and winds its way down through the Valley of Four Drafts, where the headquarters are. It's probably not the quickest or easiest way to get there, but if we follow the stream up the mountains, it'll take us where we want to go."

"But that could take days," Violet said. "We don't have a map, or any food or water for the journey, or tents or sleeping bags or any other camping equipment."

"We can use all this clothing as blankets," Klaus said, "and we can sleep in any shelter we find. There were quite a few caves on the map that animals use for hibernation."

The two Baudelaires looked at one another and shivered in the chilly breeze. The idea of hiking for hours in the mountains, only to sleep wrapped in someone else's clothing in a cave that might contain hibernating animals, was not a pleasant one, and the siblings wished they did not have to take the road less traveled, but instead could travel in a swift, well-heated vehicle and reach their sister in mere moments. But wishing, like sipping a glass of punch, or pulling aside a bearskin rug in order to access a hidden trapdoor in the floor, is merely a quiet way to spend one's time before the candles are extinguished on one's birthday cake, and the Baudelaires knew that it would be best to stop wishing and start their journey. Klaus put the hand mirror and the ukulele in his coat pockets and picked up the poncho and the pitcher, while Violet put the bread knife in her pocket and picked up the sweatshirt and the last coat, and then, with one last look at the tracks the caravan left behind as it toppled over the peak, the two children began to follow the Stricken Stream.

If you have ever traveled a long distance with a family member, then you know that there are times when you feel like talking and times when you feel like being quiet. This was one of the quiet times. Violet and Klaus walked up the slopes of the mountain toward the head-quarters they hoped to reach, and they heard the sound of the mountain winds, a low, tune-less moan like someone blowing across the top of an empty bottle, and the odd, rough sound of the stream's fish as they stuck their heads out of the dark, thick waters of the stream, but both travelers were in a quiet mood and did not say a word to one another, each lost in their own thoughts.

Violet let her mind wander to the time she had spent with her siblings in the Village of Fowl Devotees, when a mysterious man named Jacques Snicket was murdered, and the children were blamed for the crime. They had managed to escape from prison and rescue their friends Duncan and Isadora Quagmire from Count Olaf's clutches, but then had been separated at the last moment from the two triplets, who sailed away in a self-sustaining hot air mobile home built by a man named Hector. None of the Baudelaires had seen Hector or the two Quagmires since, and Violet wondered if they were safe and if they had managed to contact a secret organization they'd discovered. The organization was called V.F.D., and the Baudelaires had not yet learned exactly what the organization did, or even what all the letters stood for. The children thought that the headquarters at the Valley of Four Drafts might prove to be helpful, but now, as the eldest Baudelaire trudged alongside the Stricken Stream, she wondered if she would ever find the answers she was looking for.

Klaus was also thinking about the Quagmires, although he was thinking about when the Baudelaires first met them, at Prufrock Preparatory School. Many of the students at the school had been quite mean to the three siblings—particularly a very nasty girl named Carmelita Spats—but Isadora and Duncan had been very kind, and soon the Baudelaires and the Quag-mires had become inseparable, a word which here means "close friends." One reason for their friendship had been that both sets of children had lost people who were close to them. The Baudelaires had lost their parents, of course, and the Quagmires had lost not only their parents but their brother, the third Quagmire triplet, whose name was Quigley. Klaus thought about the Quagmires' tragedy, and felt a little guilty that one of his own parents might be alive after all. A document the Baudelaires had found con-tained a picture of their parents standing with Jacques Snicket and another man, with a cap-tion reading "Because of the evidence discussed on page nine, experts now suspect that there may in fact be one survivor of the fire, but the survivor's whereabouts are unknown." Klaus had this document in his pocket right now, along with a few scraps of the Quagmires' notebooks that they had managed to give him. Klaus walked beside his older sister, thinking of the puzzle of V.F.D. and how kindly the Quagmires had tried to help them solve the mystery that surrounded them all. He was thinking so hard about these things that when Violet finally broke the silence, it was as if he were waking up from a long, confusing dream.

"Klaus," she said, "when we were in the caravan, you said you wanted to tell me something before we tried the invention, but I didn't let you. What was it?"

"I don't know," Klaus admitted. "I just wanted to say something, in case—well, in case the invention didn't work." He sighed, and looked up at the darkening sky. "I don't remember the last thing I said to Sunny," he said quietly. "It must have been when we were in Madame Lulu's tent, or maybe outside, just before we stepped into the caravan. Had I known that Count Olaf was going to take her away, I would have tried to say something special. I could have complimented her on the hot choco-late she made, or told her how skillful she was at staying in disguise."

"You can tell her those things," Violet said, "when we see her again."

"I hope so," Klaus said glumly, "but we're so far behind Olaf and his troupe."

"But we know where they're going," Violet said, "and we know that he won't harm a hair on her head. Count Olaf thinks we perished in the caravan, so he needs Sunny to get his hands on the fortune."

"She's probably unharmed," Klaus agreed, "but I'm sure she's very frightened. I just hope she knows we're coming after her."

"Me, too," Violet said, and walked in a silence for a while, interrupted only by the wind and the odd, gurgling noise of the fish.

"I think those fish are having trouble breath-ing," Klaus said, pointing into the stream. "Something in the water is making them cough."

"Maybe the Stricken Stream isn't always

that ugly color," Violet said. "What would turn normal water into grayish black slime?"

"Iron ore," Klaus said thoughtfully, trying to remember a book on high-altitude environmentalism he had read when he was ten. "Or perhaps a clay deposit, loosened by an earthquake or another geological event, or some sort of pollution. There might be an ink or licorice factory nearby."

"Maybe V.F.D. will tell us," Violet said, "when we reach the headquarters."

"Maybe one of our parents will tell us," Klaus said quietly.

"We shouldn't get our hopes up," Violet said. "Even if one of our parents really did survive the fire, and the V.F.D. headquarters really are at the Valley of Four Drafts, we still don't know that we will see them when we arrive."

"I don't see the harm in getting our hopes up," Klaus said. "We're walking along a damaged stream, toward a vicious villain, in an attempt to rescue our sister and find the headquarters of a secret organization. I could use a little bit of hope right now."

Violet stopped in her path. "I could use another layer of clothing," she said. "It's getting colder."

Klaus nodded in agreement, and held up the garment he was carrying. "Do you want the poncho," he asked, "or the sweatshirt?"

"The poncho, if you don't mind," Violet said. "After my experience in the House of Freaks, I don't wish to advertise the Caligari Carnival."

"Me neither," Klaus said, taking the lettered sweatshirt from his sister. "I think I'll wear it inside out."

Rather than take off their coats and expose themselves to the icy winds of the Mortmain Mountains, Klaus put on the inside-out sweatshirt over his coat, and Violet wore the poncho outside hers, where it hung awkwardly around her. The two elder Baudelaires looked at one another and had to smile at their ridiculous appearance.

"These are worse than the pinstripe suits Esmé Squalor gave us," Violet said.

"Or those itchy sweaters we wore when we stayed with Mr. Poe," Klaus said, referring to a banker who was in charge of the Baudelaire fortune, with whom they had lost touch. "But at least we'll keep warm. If it gets even colder, we can take turns wearing the extra coat."

"If one of our parents is at the headquarters," Violet said, "he or she might not recognize us underneath all this clothing. We'll look like two large lumps."

The two Baudelaires looked up at the snow-covered peaks above them and felt a bit dizzy, not only from the height of the Mortmain Mountains but from all the questions buzzing around their heads. Could they really reach the Valley of Four Drafts all by themselves? What would the headquarters look like? Would V.F.D.

be expecting the Baudelaires? Would Count Olaf have reached the headquarters ahead of them? Would they find Sunny? Would they find one of their parents? Violet and Klaus looked at one another in silence and shivered in their strange clothes, until finally Klaus broke the silence with one more question, which seemed the dizziest one of all.

"Which parent," he said, "do you think is the survivor?"

Violet opened her mouth to answer, but at that moment another question immediately occupied the minds of the elder Baudelaires. It is a dreadful question, and nearly everyone who has found themselves asking it has ended up wishing that they'd never brought up the subject. My brother asked the question once, and had nightmares about it for weeks. An associate of mine asked the question, and found himself falling through the air before he could hear the answer. It is a question I asked once, a very long time ago and in a very timid voice, and a woman replied by quickly putting a motorcycle helmet on her head and wrapping her body in a red silk cape. The question is, "What in the world is that ominous-looking cloud of tiny, white buzzing objects coming toward us?" and I'm sorry to tell you that the answer is "A swarm of well-organized, ill-tempered insects known as snow gnats, who live in cold mountain areas and enjoy stinging people for no reason whatsoever."

"What in the world," Violet said, "is that ominous-looking cloud of tiny, white buzzing objects coming toward us?"

Klaus looked in the direction his sister was pointing and frowned. "I remember reading something in a book on mountainous insect life," he said, "but I can't quite recall the details."

"Try to remember," Violet said, looking nervously at the approaching swarm. The ominous-looking cloud of tiny, white buzzing objects had appeared from around a rocky corner, and from a distance it looked a bit like the beginnings of a snowfall. But now the snowfall was organizing itself into the shape of an arrow, and moving toward the two children, buzzing louder and louder as if it were annoyed. "I think they might be snow gnats," Klaus said. "Snow gnats live in cold mountain areas and have been known to group themselves into well-defined shapes."

Violet looked from the approaching arrow to the waters of the stream and the steep edge of the mountain peak. "I'm glad gnats are harmless," she said. "It doesn't look like there's any way to avoid them."

"There's something else about snow gnats," Klaus said, "that I'm not quite remembering."

The swarm drew quite close, with the tip of the fluttering white arrow just a few inches from the Baudelaires' noses, and then stopped in its path, buzzing angrily. The two siblings stood face-to-face with the snow gnats for a long, tense second, and the gnat at the very, very tip of the arrow flew daintily forward and stung Violet on the nose.

"Ow!" Violet said. The snow gnat flew back

to its place, and the eldest Baudelaire was left rubbing a tiny red mark on her nose. "That hurt," she said. "It feels like a pin stuck me."

"I remember now," Klaus said. "Snow gnats are ill-tempered and enjoy stinging people for no reason whatso—"

But Klaus did not get to finish his sentence, because the snow gnats interrupted and gave a ghastly demonstration of just what he was talking about. Curling lazily in the mountain winds, the arrow twisted and became a large buzzing circle, and the gnats began to spin around and around the two Baudelaires like a well-organized and ill-tempered hula hoop. Each gnat was so tiny that the children could not see any of its features, but they felt as if the insects were smiling nastily.

"Are the stings poisonous?" Violet asked.

"Mildly," Klaus said. "We'll be all right if we get stung a few times, but many stings could make us very ill. Ow!"

One of the gnats had flown up and stung

Klaus on the cheek, as if it were seeing if the middle Baudelaire was fun to hurt. "People always say that if you don't bother stinging insects, they won't bother you," Violet said nervously. "Ow!"

"That's scarcely ever true," Klaus said, "and it's certainly not true with snow gnats. Ow! Ow! *Ow!*"

"What should we—*Ow!*" Violet half asked.

"I don't—*Ow!*" Klaus half answered, but in moments the Baudelaires did not have time for even half a conversation. The circle of snow gnats began spinning faster and faster, and the insects spread themselves out so it looked as if the two siblings were in the middle of a tiny, white tornado. Then, in a series of manuevers that must have taken a great deal of rehearsal, the gnats began stinging the Baudelaires, first on one side and then on the other. Violet shrieked as several gnats stung her chin. Klaus shouted as a handful of gnats stung his left ear. And both Baudelaires cried out as they tried to wave the gnats away only to feel the stingers all over their waving hands. The snow gnats stung to the left, and stung to the right. They approached the Baudelaires from above, making the children duck, and then from below, making the children stand on tiptoe in an effort to avoid them. And all the while, the swarm buzzed louder and louder, as if wishing to remind the Baudelaires how much fun the insects were having. Violet and Klaus closed their eyes and stood together, too scared to walk blindly and find themselves falling off a mountain peak or sinking into the waters of the Stricken Stream.

"Coat!" Klaus managed to shout, then spit out a gnat that had flown into his open mouth in the hopes of stinging his tongue. Violet understood at once, and grabbed the extra coat in her hands and draped it over Klaus and herself like a large, limp umbrella of cloth. The snow gnats buzzed furiously, trying to get inside to continue stinging them, but had to settle for stinging the Baudelaires' hands as they held the coat in place.

Violet and Klaus looked at one another dimly underneath the coat, wincing as their fingers were stung, and tried to keep walking.

"We'll never reach the Valley of Four Drafts like this," Violet said, speaking louder than usual over the buzzing of the gnats. "How can we stop them, Klaus?"

"Fire drives them away," Klaus said. "In the book I read, the author said that even the smell of smoke can keep a whole swarm at bay. But we can't start a fire underneath a coat."

"Ow!" A snow gnat stung Violet's thumb on a spot that had already been stung, just as the Baudelaires rounded the rocky corner where the swarm had first appeared. Through a worn spot in the fabric, the Baudelaires could just make out a dark, circular hole in the side of the mountain.

"That must be an entrance to one of the caves," Klaus said. "Could we start a fire in there?"

"Maybe," Violet said. "And maybe we'd annoy a hibernating animal."

"We've already managed to annoy thousands of animals," Klaus said, almost dropping the pitcher as a gnat stung his wrist. "I don't think we have much choice. I think we have to head into the cave and take our chances."

Violet nodded in agreement, but looked nervously at the entrance to the cave. Taking one's chances is like taking a bath, because sometimes you end up feeling comfortable and warm, and sometimes there is something terrible lurking around that you cannot see until it is too late and you can do nothing else but scream and cling to a plastic duck. The two Baudelaires walked carefully toward the dark, circular hole, making sure to stay clear of the nearby edge of the peak and pulling the coat tightly around them so the snow gnats could not find a way inside, but what worried them most was not the height of the peak or the stingers of the gnats but the chances they were taking as they ducked inside the gloomy entrance of the cave.

The two Baudelaires had never been in this

cave before, of course, and as far as I have been able to ascertain, they were never in it again, even on their way back down the mountain, after they had been reunited with their baby sister and learned the secret of Verbal Fridge Dialogue. And yet, as Violet and Klaus took their chances and walked inside, they found two things with which they were familiar. The first was fire. As they stood inside the entrance to the cave, the siblings realized at once that there was no need to worry about the snow gnats any longer, because they could smell nearby smoke, and even see, at a great distance, small orange flames toward the back of the cave. Fire, of course, was very familiar to the children, from the ashen smell of the remains of the Baudelaire mansion to the scent of the flames that destroyed Caligari Carnival. But as the snow gnats formed an arrow and darted away from the cave and the Baudelaires took another step inside, Violet and Klaus found another familiar thing—a familiar person, to be exact, who they had thought they would never see again.

"Hey you cakesniffers!" said a voice from the back of the cave, and the sound was almost enough to make the two Baudelaires wish they had taken their chances someplace else.

CHAPTER
Three

You may well wonder why there has been no account of Sunny Baudelaire in the first two chapters of this book, but there are several reasons why this is so. For one thing, Sunny's journey in Count Olaf's car was much more difficult to research. The tracks made by the tires of the car have vanished long ago, and so many blizzards and avalanches have occurred in the Mortmain Mountains that even the road itself has largely disappeared. The few witnesses to Olaf's journey have mostly died under mysterious circumstances, or were too frightened to answer the letters, telegrams, and greeting cards I sent them requesting an interview. And even the litter that was thrown out the window of Olaf's car—the clearest sign that evil people have driven by—was picked up off the road long before my work began. The missing litter is a good sign, as it indicates that certain animals of the Mortmain Mountains have returned to their posts and are rebuilding their nests, but it has made it very hard for me to write a complete account of Sunny's travels.

But if you are interested in knowing how Sunny Baudelaire spent her time while her siblings stopped the caravan, followed the path of the Stricken Stream, and struggled against the snow gnats, there is another story you might read that describes more or less the same situation. The story concerns a person named Cinderella. Cinderella was a young person who was placed in the care of various wicked people who teased her and forced her to do all the chores. Eventually Cinderella was rescued by her fairy godmother, who magically created a special outfit for Cinderella to wear to a ball where she met a handsome prince, married him soon afterward, and lived happily ever after in a castle. If you substitute the name "Cinderella" with the name "Sunny Baudelaire," and eliminate the fairy godmother, the special outfit, the ball, the handsome prince, the marriage, and living happily ever after in a castle, you will have a clear idea of Sunny's predicament.

"I wish the baby orphan would stop that irritating crying," Count Olaf said, wrinkling his one eyebrow as the car made another violent turn. "Nothing spoils a nice car trip like a whiny kidnapping victim."

"I'm pinching her as often as I can," Esmé Squalor said, and gave Sunny another pinch with her stylish fingernails, "but she still won't shut up."

"Listen, toothy," Olaf said, taking his eyes off the road to glare at Sunny. "If you don't stop crying, I'll give you something to cry about."

Sunny gave a little whimper of annoyance, and wiped her eyes with her tiny hands. It was

true that she had been crying for most of the
day, thoroughout a long drive that even the most
dedicated of researchers would be unable to
trace, and now as the sun set, she still had not
been able to stop herself. But at Count Olaf's
words, she was almost more irritated than frightened. It is always tedious when someone says
that if you don't stop crying, they will give you
something to cry about, because if you are crying than you already have something to cry
about, and so there is no reason for them to give
you anything additional to cry about, thank you
very much. Sunny Baudelaire certainly felt she
had sufficient reason to weep. She was worried
about her siblings, and wondered how they were
going to stop the runaway caravan from hurtling
them to their doom. She was frightened for herself, now that Count Olaf had discovered her
disguise, torn off her beard, and trapped her on
Esmé's lap. And she was in pain, from the con-
stant pinching of the villain's girlfriend. "No
pinch," she said to Esmé, but the wicked and

stylish woman just frowned as if Sunny had spoken nonsense.

"When she's not crying," Esmé said, "the baby talks in some foreign language. I can't understand a thing she's saying."

"Kidnapped children are never any fun," said the hook-handed man, who was perhaps Sunny's least favorite of Olaf's troupe. "Remember when we had the Quagmires in our clutches, boss? They did nothing but complain. They complained when we put them in a cage. They complained when we trapped them inside a fountain. Complain, complain, complain—I was so sick of them I was almost glad when they escaped from our clutches."

"Glad?" Count Olaf said with a snarl. "We worked hard to steal the Quagmire fortune, and we didn't get a single sapphire. That was a real waste of time."

"Don't blame yourself, Olaf," said one of the white-faced women from the back scat. "Everybody makes mistakes."

"Not this time," Olaf said. "With the two orphans squashed someplace underneath a crashed caravan and the baby orphan on your lap, the Baudelaire fortune is mine. And once we reach the Valley of Four Drafts and find the headquarters, all our worries will be over."

"Why?" asked Hugo, the hunchbacked man who had previously been employed at the carnival.

"Yes, please explain," said Kevin, another former carnival worker. At Caligari Carnival, Kevin had been embarrassed to be ambidextrous, but Esmé had lured him into joining Olaf's troupe by tying Kevin's right hand behind his back, so no one would know it was as strong as his left. "Remember, boss, we're new to the troupe, so we don't always know what's going on."

"I remember when I first joined Olaf's troupe," the other white-faced woman said. "I'd never even heard of the Snicket file."

"Working for me is a hands-on learning

experience," Olaf said. "You can't rely on me to explain everything to you. I'm a very busy man."

"I'll explain it, boss," said the hook-handed man. "Count Olaf, like any good businessman, has committed a wide variety of crimes."

"But these stupid volunteers have gathered all sorts of evidence and filed it away," Esmé said. "I tried to explain that crime is very in right now, but apparently they weren't interested."

Sunny wiped another tear from her eye and sighed. The youngest Baudelaire thought she'd almost rather be pinched again than hear any more of Esmé Squalor's nonsense about what was in—the word that Esmé used for "fashionable"—and what was out.

"We need to destroy those files, or Count Olaf could be arrested," the hook-handed man said. "We have reason to believe that some of the files are at V.F.D. headquarters."

"What does V.F.D. stand for?" The voice of Colette came from the floor of the automobile.

Count Olaf had ordered her to use her skills as a carnival contortionist to curl up at the feet of the other members of the troupe.

"That's top-secret information!" Olaf growled, to Sunny's disappointment. "I used to be a member of the organization myself, but I found it was more fun to be an individual practitioner."

"What does that mean?" asked the hook-handed man.

"It means a life of crime," Esmé replied. "It's very in right now."

"Wrong def." Sunny could not help speaking through her tears. By "wrong def" she meant something along the lines of, "An individual practitioner means someone who works alone, instead of with a group, and it has nothing to do with a life of crime," and it made her sad that there was no one around who could understand her.

"There you go, babbling away," Esmé said. "This is why I never want to have children.

Except as servants, of course."

"This journey is easier than I thought," Olaf said. "The map says we just have to pass a few more caves."

"Is there an in hotel near the headquarters?" Esmé asked.

"I'm afraid not, sweetheart," the villain replied, "but I have two tents in the trunk of the car. We'll be camping on Mount Fraught, the summit of the Mortmain Mountains."

"The summit?" Esmé said. "It'll be cold at the highest peak."

"It's true," Olaf admitted, "but False Spring is on its way, so before long it'll be a bit warmer."

"But what about tonight?" Esmé Squalor said. "It is definitely *not* in for me to set up tents in the freezing cold."

Count Olaf looked at his girlfriend and began to laugh, and Sunny could smell the foul breath of his nasty giggles. "Don't be silly," the villain said finally. "*You're* not going to set up the tents, Esmé. You're going to stay nice and toasty in the car. The bucktoothed baby will set up the tents for us."

Now Olaf's entire troupe laughed, and the car filled with the stench of so many villains' bad breath. Sunny felt a few more tears roll down her face, and turned to the window so no one would see. The car's windows were very dirty, but the youngest Baudelaire could see the strange, square peaks of the Mortmain Mountains and the dark waters of the Stricken Stream. By now the car had driven so high up in the mountains that the stream was mostly ice, and Sunny looked at the wide stripe of frozen blackness and wondered where her siblings were, and if they were coming to rescue her. She remembered the other time she had been in Count Olaf's clutches, when the villain had tied her up, locked her in a cage and dangled her outside his tower room as part of one of his schemes. It had been an absolutely terrifying experience for the youngest Baudelaire, and she often still had nightmares about the creaking of the cage and the distant sight of her two siblings looking up at her from Count Olaf's backyard. But Violet had built a grappling hook to rescue her, and Klaus had done some important legal research to defeat Olaf's scheme. As the car took Sunny farther and farther away from her siblings, and she stared out at the lonesome terrain, she knew that they could save her again.

"How long will we stay on Mount Fraught?" Hugo asked.

"Until I say so, of course," Count Olaf replied.

"You'll soon find out that much of this job involves a lot of waiting around," the hook-handed man said. "I usually keep something around to help pass the time, like a deck of cards or a large rock."

"It can be dull," admitted one of the white-faced women, "and it can be dangerous. Several of our comrades have recently suffered terrible fates."

"It was worth it," Count Olaf said nonchalantly, a word which here means "in a tone of voice that indicated he didn't care one bit about his deceased employees." "Sometimes a few people need to die in fires or get eaten by lions, if it's all for the greater good."

"What's the greater good?" asked Colette.

"Money!" Esmé cried in greedy glee. "Money and personal satisfaction, and we're going to get both of those things out of this whimpering baby on my lap! Once we have our hands on the Baudelaire fortune, we'll have enough money to live a life of luxury and plan several more treacherous schemes!"

The entire troupe cheered, and Count Olaf gave Sunny a filthy grin, but did not say anything more as the car raced up a steep, bumpy hill, and at last screeched to a halt, just as the last rays of the sun faded into the evening sky. "We're here at last," Count Olaf said, and handed the car keys to Sunny. "Get out, baby orphan. Unload everything from the trunk and set up the tents."

"And bring us some potato chips," Esmé said, "so we'll have something in to eat while we wait."

Esmé opened the door of the car, placed Sunny on the frozen ground, and slammed the door shut again. Instantly, the chilly mountain air surrounded the youngest Baudelaire and made her shiver. It was so bitterly cold at the highest peak of the Mortmain Mountains that her tears froze in their tracks, forming a tiny mask of ice all over her face. Unsteadily, Sunny rose to her feet and walked to the back of the car. She was tempted to keep walking, and escape from Olaf while he waited in the car with his troupe. But where could she go? Sunny looked around at her surroundings and could not see a place where a baby would be safe by herself.

The summit of Mount Fraught was a small,

flat square, and as Sunny walked to the trunk of the car, she gazed off each edge of the square, feeling a bit dizzy from the great height. From three of the edges, she could see the square and misty peaks of some of the other mountains, most of which were covered in snow, and twisting through the peaks were the strange, black waters of the Stricken Stream, and the rocky path that the car had driven along. But from the fourth side of the square peak, Sunny saw something so strange it took her a moment to figure out what it was.

Extending from the highest peak in the Mortmain Mountains was a glittering white strip, like an enormous piece of shiny paper folded downward, or the wing of some tremendous bird. Sunny watched the very last rays of the sunset reflect off this enormous surface and slowly realized what it was: the source of the Stricken Stream. Like many streams, the Stricken Stream originated within the rocks of the mountains, and in the warmer season, Sunny could see that it cascaded down from the highest peak in an enormous waterfall. But this was not a warm time of year, and just as Sunny's tears had frozen on her face, the waterfall had frozen solid, into a long, slippery slope that disappeared into the darkness below. It was such an eerie sight that it took Sunny a moment to wonder why the ice was white, instead of black like the waters of the Stricken Stream.

Honk! A loud blast from Count Olaf's horn made Sunny remember what she was supposed to be doing, and she hurriedly opened the trunk and found a bag of potato chips, which she brought back to the car. "That took a very long time, orphan," said Olaf, rather than "Thank you." "Now go set up the tents, one for Esmé and me and one for my troupe, so we can get some sleep."

"Where is the baby going to stay?" asked the hook-handed man. "I don't want her in my tent. I hear that babies can creep up and steal your breath while you're sleeping."

"Well, she's certainly not sleeping with me," Esmé said. "It's not in to have a baby in your tent."

"She's not going to sleep in either tent," Olaf decided. "There's a large covered casserole dish in the trunk. She can sleep in there."

"Will she be safe in a casserole dish?" Esmé said. "Remember, Olaf honey, if she dies then we can't get our hands on the fortune."

"There are a few holes in the top so she can breathe," Olaf said, "and the cover will protect her from the snow gnats."

"Snow gnats?" asked Hugo.

"Snow gnats are well-organized, ill-tempered insects," Count Olaf explained, "who live in cold mountain areas and enjoy stinging people for no reason whatsoever. I've always been fond of them."

"Nonat," Sunny said, which meant "I didn't notice any such insects outside," but no one paid any attention.

"Won't she run away if no one's watching her?" asked Kevin.

"She wouldn't dare," Count Olaf said, "and even if she tried to survive in the mountains by herself, we could see where she went. That's why we're staying here at the summit. We'll know if the brat escapes, or if anyone's coming after us, because we can see everything and everyone for miles and miles."

"Eureka," Sunny said, before she could stop herself. She meant something along the lines of, "I've just realized something," but she had not meant to say it out loud.

"Stop your babbling and get busy, you fanged brat!" Esmé Squalor said, and slammed the car door shut. Sunny could hear the laughing of the troupe and the crunching of potato chips as she walked slowly back to the trunk to find the tents.

It is often quite frustrating to arrange all of the cloth and the poles so that a tent works correctly, which is why I have always preferred to stay in hotels or rented castles, which also have the added attractions of solid walls and maid service. Sunny, of course, had the extra disadvantages of trying to do it herself, in the dark, when she was still fairly new at walking and was worried about her siblings. But the youngest Baudelaire had a history of performing Herculean tasks, a phrase which here means "managing to do incredibly difficult things." As I'm sure you know, if you are ever forced to do something very difficult, it often helps to think of something inspiring to keep you going. When Sunny had engaged in a sword-and-tooth fight at Lucky Smells Lumbermill, for instance, she thought of how much she cared for her siblings, and it helped her defeat the evil Dr. Orwell. When Sunny climbed up an elevator shaft at 667 Dark Avenue, she had concentrated on her friends the Quagmires, and how much she wanted to rescue them, and before too long she had reached the penthouse apartment. So, as

Sunny dug a hole in the frozen ground with her teeth so the tent poles would stay in place, she thought of something that inspired her, and oddly enough it was something that Count Olaf had said, about being able to see everything and everyone for miles and miles. As Sunny assembled the tents, and gazed down every so often at the slippery slope of the frozen waterfall, she decided that she would not try to sneak away from Olaf and his troupe. She would not to try to sneak anywhere. Because if you could see everything and everyone from Mount Fraught, that also meant everything and everyone, including Violet and Klaus Baudelaire, would be able to see her.

CHAPTER Four

That night was a dark day. Of course, all nights are dark days, because night is simply a badly lit version of day, due to the fact that the Earth travels around and around the sun reminding everyone that it is time to get out of bed and start the day with a cup of coffee or a secret message folded up into a paper airplane that can sail out the barred window of a ranger station. But in this case,

the phrase "a dark day" means "a sad time in the history of the Baudelaire children, V.F.D., and all kind, brave, and well-read people in the world." But Violet and Klaus Baudelaire, of course, had no idea of the catastrophe occurring high above them in the Valley of Four Drafts. All they knew was that they were hearing a voice they had hoped never to hear again.

"Go away, cakesniffers!" the voice said. "This is a private cave!"

"Who are you talking to, Carmelita?" asked another voice. This voice was much louder, and sounded like it belonged to a grown man.

"I can see two shadows in the entrance of the cave, Uncle Bruce," said the first voice, "and to me they look like cakesniffers."

The back of the cave echoed with giggling, and Violet and Klaus looked at one another in dismay. The familiar voice belonged to Carmelita Spats, the nasty little girl whom the Baudelaires had encountered at Prufrock Preparatory School. Carmelita had taken an instant dislike to the three siblings, calling them unpleasant names and generally making life miserable at the academy. If you have ever been a student, then you know that there is usually one such person at every school and that once you have graduated you hope never to see them again. The two elder Baudelaires had enough troubles in the Mortmain Mountains without running into this unpleasant person, and at the sound of her voice they almost turned around and took their chances once more with the snow gnats swarming outside.

"Two shadows?" asked the second voice. "Identify yourselves, please."

"We're mountain travelers," Violet called from the entrance. "We lost our way and ran into a swarm of snow gnats. Please let us rest here for a moment, while the smell of smoke scares them away, and then we'll be on our way."

"Absolutely not!" replied Carmelita, who sounded even nastier than usual. "This is where the Snow Scouts are camping, on their way to celebrate False Spring and crown me queen. We don't want any cakesniffers spoiling our fun."

"Now, now, Carmelita," said the voice of the grown man. "Snow Scouts are supposed to be accommodating, remember? It's part of the Snow Scout Alphabet Pledge. And it would be very accommodating of us to offer these strangers the shelter of our cave."

"I don't want to be accommodating," Carmelita said. "I'm the False Spring Queen, so I get to do whatever I want."

"You're not the False Spring Queen yet, Carmelita," came the patient voice of a young boy. "Not until we dance around the Springpole. Do come in, travelers, and sit by the fire. We're happy to accommodate you."

"That's the spirit, kid," said the voice of the grown man. "Come on, Snow Scouts, let's all say the Snow Scout Alphabet Pledge together."

Instantly the cave echoed with the sound of many voices speaking in perfect unison, a phrase which here means "reciting a list of very odd words at the very same time." "Snow Scouts," recited the Snow Scouts, "are accommodating, basic, calm, darling, emblematic, frisky, grinning, human, innocent, jumping, kept, limited, meek, nap-loving, official, pretty, quarantined, recent, scheduled, tidy, understandable, victorious, wholesome, xylophone, young, and zippered—every morning, every afternoon, every night, and all day long!"

The two Baudelaires looked at one another in confusion. Like many pledges, the Snow Scout Alphabet Pledge had not made much sense, and Violet and Klaus tried to imagine how a scout could be "calm" and "meek" at the same time as being "frisky" and "jumping," or how all these children could avoid being "young" or "human," even if they wanted to. They couldn't figure out why the pledge suggested being all these things "every morning," "every afternoon," and "every night," and then added "all day long," or why the word "xylophone" appeared in the pledge at all. But they

A SERIES OF UNFORTUNATE EVENTS

did not have much time to wonder, because when the pledge was over, the Snow Scouts all took a big breath and made a long, airy sound, as if they were imitating the wind outside, and this seemed even more strange.

"That's my favorite part," said the voice of the grown man, when the sound faded away. "There's nothing like ending the Snow Scout Alphabet Pledge with a snowy sound. Now approach, travelers, so we can get a look at you."

"Let's keep the coat over our faces," Klaus whispered to his sister. "Carmelita might recognize us."

"And the other scouts have probably seen our pictures in *The Daily Punctilio*," Violet said, and ducked her head underneath the coat. *The Daily Punctilio* was a newspaper that had published a story blaming the three Baudelaires for Jacques Snicket's murder. The story was utter nonsense, of course, but it seemed that everyone in the world had believed it and was searching for the Baudelaires to put them in jail. As

the two siblings walked toward the voices of the
Snow Scouts, however, they realized that they
weren't the only ones concealing their faces.

The back of the cave was like a large, circular room, with very high ceilings and craggy
walls of rock that flickered in the orange light
of the flames. Seated in a circle around the fire
were fifteen or twenty people, all looking up at
the two Baudelaires. Through the fabric of the
coat, the children could see that one person was
much taller than the others—this was probably
Bruce—and was wearing an ugly plaid coat and
holding a large cigar. On the opposite side of the
circle was someone wearing a thick wool
sweater with several large pockets, and the rest
of the Snow Scouts were wearing bright white
uniforms with enormous zippers down the front
and emblems of snowflakes, in all different sizes
and shapes, along the long, puffy sleeves. On
the back of the uniforms, the Baudelaires could
see the words of the Snow Scout Alphabet
Pledge printed in large pink letters, and on the

top of everyone's heads were white headbands with tiny plastic snowflakes sticking out of the top in all directions and the word "Brr!" written in icy script. But Violet and Klaus weren't looking at the plastic flurries of snow on the Snow Scouts' heads, or the accommodating, basic, calm, darling, emblematic, frisky, grinning, human, innocent, jumping, kept, limited, meek, nap-loving, official, pretty, quarantined, recent, scheduled, tidy, understandable, victorious, wholesome, xylophone, young, and zippered uniforms that most everyone was wearing. They were looking at the dark, round masks that were covering the scouts' faces. The masks were covered in tiny holes, much like masks worn for fencing, a sport in which people swordfight for fun rather than for honor or in order to rescue a writer who has been taped to the wall. But in the flickering light of the cave, the Baudelaires could not see the holes, and it looked like the faces of Bruce and the Snow Scouts had vanished, leaving a dark and empty hole above their necks.

"You cakesniffers look ridiculous," said one of the scouts, and the Baudelaires knew at once which masked figure was Carmelita Spats. "Your faces are all covered up."

"We're meek," Violet said, thinking quickly. "In fact, we're so meek that we hardly ever show our faces."

"Then you'll fit in just fine," said Bruce from behind his mask. "The name's Bruce, but you can call me Uncle Bruce, although I'm almost certainly not your real uncle. Welcome to the Snow Scouts, travelers, where all of us are meek. In fact, we're accommodating, basic, calm . . ."

The other Snow Scouts all joined in the pledge, and the two elder Baudelaires stood through another rendition of the absurd list, while the scout in the sweater stood up and stepped toward them. "We have some spare masks over there," he murmured quietly, and gestured toward a large pile of equipment, stacked beside a very long wooden pole. "They'll keep the snow gnats away when you go back outside. Help yourself."

"Thank you," Violet replied, as the scouts promised to be kept, limited, and meek. She and her brother quickly grabbed masks and put them on underneath the coat, so that by the time the scouts vowed to be xylophone, young, and zippered, they looked as faceless as everyone else in the cave.

"That was fun, kids," said Bruce, as the snowy sound faded and the pledge was over. "Now why don't you two join the Snow Scouts? We're an organization for young people to have fun and learn new things. Right now we're on a Snow Scout Hike. We're going to hike all the way up to Mount Fraught in order to celebrate False Spring."

"What's False Spring?" Violet asked, sitting down between her brother and the sweatered scout.

"Anybody who's not a cakesniffer knows what False Spring is," Carmelita said in a scornful voice. "It's when the weather gets unusually warm before getting very cold again. We celebrate it with a fancy dance where we spin around and around the Springpole." She pointed to the wooden pole, and the Baudelaires noticed that the Snow Scouts all wore bright white mittens, each emblazoned with an S. "When the dance is over, we choose the best Snow Scout and crown her the False Spring Queen. This time, it's me. In fact, it's always me."

"That's because Uncle Bruce is really your uncle," said one of the other Snow Scouts.

"No, it's not," Carmelita insisted. "It's because I'm the most accommodating, basic, calm, darling, emblematic, frisky, grinning, human, innocent, jumping, kept, limited, meek, nap-loving, official, pretty, quarantined, recent, scheduled, tidy, understandable, victorious, wholesome, xylophone, young, and zippered."

"How can anyone be 'xylophone'?" Klaus

couldn't help asking. "'Xylophone' isn't even an adjective."

"Uncle Bruce couldn't think of another word that began with X," explained the sweatered Snow Scout, in a tone of voice indicating that he thought this wasn't a very good excuse.

"How about 'xenial'?" Klaus suggested. "It's a word that means—"

"You can't change the words of the Snow Scout Alphabet Pledge," Bruce interrupted, moving his cigar toward his face as if he were going to try to smoke it through the mask. "The whole point of the Snow Scouts is that you do the same thing over and over. We celebrate False Spring over and over, on Mount Fraught, at the source of the Stricken Stream. My niece Carmelita Spats is False Spring Queen, over and over. And over and over, we stop here in this cave for Snow Scout Story Time."

"I read that the caves of the Mortmain Mountains contained hibernating animals," Klaus said. "Are you sure it's safe to stop here?"

The Snow Scout who was wearing a sweater instead of a uniform turned his head quickly to the Baudelaires, as if he was going to speak, but Bruce answered first. "It's safe now, kid," he said. "Years ago, apparently these mountains were crawling with bears. The bears were so intelligent that they were trained as soldiers. But they disappeared and no one knows why."

"Not bears," the scout in the sweater said, so quietly that the two Baudelaires had to lean in to hear him. "Lions lived in these caves. And they weren't soldiers. The lions were detectives—volunteer feline detectives." He turned so his mask was facing the two siblings, and the children knew he must be staring at them through the holes. "Volunteer Feline Detectives," he said again, and the Baudelaires almost gasped.

"Did you say—" Violet said, but the sweatered Snow Scout shook his head as if it was not safe to talk. Violet looked at her brother and then at the scout, wishing she could see both of their faces behind their masks. The initials of "Volunteer Feline Detectives," of course, spelled "V.F.D.," the name of the organization they were looking for. But were these initials a coincidence, as they had seemed to be so many times? Or was this mysterious scout giving them some sort of signal?

"I don't know what you kids are muttering about," Bruce said, "but stop it this instant. It's not time for conversation. It's Snow Scout Story Time, when one Snow Scout tells a story to the other Snow Scouts. Then we'll all eat marshmallows until we feel sick and go to sleep on a heap of blankets, just like we do every year. Why don't our new scouts tell the first story?"

"I should tell the first story," whined Carmelita. "After all, I'm the False Spring Queen."

"But I'm sure the travelers will have a wonderful story to tell," the sweatered scout said. "I'd love to hear a Very Fascinating Drama."

Klaus saw his sister raise her hands to her

head and smiled. He knew Violet had instinc-
tively begun to tie her hair up in a ribbon to help
her think, but it was impossible to do so with a
mask on. Both the Baudelaire minds were racing to figure out a way to communicate with this
mysterious scout, and the children were so lost
in thought that they scarcely heard Carmelita
Spats insulting them.

"Stop sitting around, cakesniffers," Carmelita
said. "If you're going to tell us a story, get started."

"I'm sorry for the delay," Violet said, choosing her words as carefully as she could. "We
haven't had a Very Fun Day, so it's difficult to
think of a good story."

"I didn't realize this was a sad occasion,"
said the sweatered scout.

"Oh, yes," Klaus said. "We've had nothing
to eat all day except for some Vinegar-Flavored
Doughnuts."

"And then there were the snow gnats," Violet said. "They behaved like Violent Frozen
Dragonflies."

"When they form an arrow," Klaus said, "they're more like a Voracious Fierce Dragon."

"Or a Vain Fat Dictator, I imagine," the scout in the sweater said, and gave the Baudelaires a masked nod as if he had received their message.

"This is the most boring story I have ever heard," Carmelita Spats said. "Uncle Bruce, tell these two that they're both cakesniffers."

"Well, it wouldn't be very accommodating to say so," Bruce said, "but I must admit that the story you were telling was a little dull, kids. When Snow Scouts tell stories, they skip everything boring and only tell the interesting parts. That way, the story can be as accommodating, basic, calm, darling, emblematic, frisky, grinning, human, innocent, jumping, kept, limited, meek, nap-loving, official, pretty, quarantined, recent, scheduled, tidy, understandable, victorious, wholesome, xylophone, young, and zippered as possible."

"I'll show these cakesniffers how to tell an

interesting story," Carmelita said. "Once upon
a time, I woke up and looked in the mirror, and
there I saw the prettiest, smartest, most darling
girl in the whole wide world. I put on a lovely
pink dress to make myself look even prettier,
and I skipped off to school where my teacher
told me I looked more adorable than anyone she
had ever seen in her entire life, and she gave me
a lollipop as a special present . . ."

At this point, I will take a page from someone's book, a phrase which here means "adopt
an idea used by somebody else." If, for instance,
a man told you that the best way to write thank-
you notes is to reward yourself with a cookie
every time you finished one, you might take a
page from his book, and have a plate of cookies
nearby after your birthday or some other gift-
giving occasion. If a girl told you that the best
way to sneak out of the house late at night is to
make sure everyone else is sound asleep, you
might take a page from her book and mix a
sleeping potion into everyone else's after-

dinner coffee before climbing down the ivy that grows outside your bedroom window. And if you have been reading this miserable story, then the next time you find yourself in a similar situation, you might take a page from *The Slippery Slope* and use a combination of sticky substances and a drag chute to slow down a racing caravan, and then retrieve several articles of heavy clothing in order to protect yourself from the cold, and find a cave full of Snow Scouts gathered around a fire when the snow gnats begin to swarm.

But I will be taking a page from Bruce's book, when he suggested that a storyteller only tell the interesting parts of the story and skip everything boring. Certainly the two elder Baudelaires wished they could skip this boring part of their own story, as they were very eager to leave the cave and resume their search for their sister. But Violet and Klaus knew that they shouldn't leave the cave until they could talk to the mysterious boy in the sweater, and that they couldn't talk to the mysterious boy in the sweater in front of Bruce and the other Snow Scouts, and so they sat by the fire as Carmelita Spats talked on and on about how pretty and smart and darling she was and how everyone she met told her that she was unbelievably adorable. Although the Baudelaires had to sit through these tedious portions of their story, there is no reason for you to do so, and so I will skip ahead, past the tiresome details of Carmelita's endless story, and the senseless pledge that Bruce made everyone say several more times, and the all-marshmallow meal that the scouts shared with the two siblings. I will skip how irksome it was for Violet and Klaus to turn away from the scouts, quickly lift their masks, and pop marsh-mallows into their mouths before covering their faces again so they would not be recognized. After their long, tiring journey, the children would have preferred a more substantial supper and a less complicated way of eating it, but the siblings could not skip these parts of their story, so they had to wait for the evening to pass and for all the other Snow Scouts to feel sick and arrange blankets into a large heap beside the Springpole. Even when Bruce led the Snow Scouts in one more alphabet pledge as a way of saying good night, Violet and Klaus dared not get up and talk to the sweatered scout for fear of being overheard, and they had to wait for hours, too curious and anxious to sleep, as the fire died down and the cave echoed with the sounds of Snow Scout snoring. But I will take a page from the book of the Snow Scout leader, and skip ahead to the next interesting thing that happened, which was very, very late at night, when so many interesting parts of stories happen and so many people miss them because they are asleep in their beds, or hiding in the broom closet of a mustard factory, disguised as a dustpan to fool the night watchwoman.

It was very late at night—in fact one might say that it was the darkest part of this dark day—and it was so late that the Baudelaires had almost given up on staying awake, particularly after such an exhausting day, but just as the two siblings were beginning to fall asleep, they each felt a hand touch them on the shoulder, and they quickly sat up and found themselves look-ing into the masked face of the sweatered scout.

"Come with me, Baudelaires," the boy said in a very quiet voice. "I know a shortcut to the headquarters," and this was an interesting part of the story indeed.

CHAPTER
Five

When you have many questions on your mind, and you suddenly have an opportunity to ask them, the questions tend to crowd together and trip over one another, much like passengers on a crowded train when it reaches a popular station. With Bruce and the Snow Scouts asleep, the two elder Baudelaires finally had an opportunity to talk with the mysterious scout in the sweater, but everything they wanted to ask seemed hopelessly entangled.

"How—" Violet started, but the question "How did you know we were the Baudelaires?" stumbled against the question "Who are you?" and fell back against the questions "Are you a member of V.F.D.?" and "What does V.F.D. stand for?"

"Do—" Klaus said, but the question "Do you know where our sister is?" tripped over the question "Do you know if one of our parents is alive?" which was already struggling with "How can we get to the headquarters?" and "Will my sisters and I ever find a safe place to live without constantly being threatened by Count Olaf and his troupe as they hatch plan after plan to steal the Baudelaire fortune?" although the middle Baudelaire knew that his last question was unlikely to be answered at all.

"I'm sure you have lots of questions," the boy whispered, "but we can't talk here. Bruce is a light sleeper, and he's caused V.F.D. enough trouble already without learning another of our secrets. I promise all your questions will be answered, but first we've got to get to the head-quarters. Come with me."

Without another word, the sweatered scout turned around, and the Baudelaires saw he was wearing a backpack inscribed with an insignia they had seen at Caligari Carnival. At first glance, this insignia merely appeared to be an eye, but the children had discovered that if you looked closely you could see the initials V.F.D. cleverly hidden in the drawing. The scout began to walk, and the two siblings got out of their blankets as quietly as they could and followed him. To their surprise, he did not lead them toward the cave entrance, but to the back of the cave, where the Snow Scouts' fire had been. Now it was nothing more than a pile of gray ashes, although it was still very warm, and the smell of smoke was still in the air. The sweatered scout reached into his pocket and brought out a flashlight. "I had to wait for the fire to die down before I showed you," he said, and with a nervous glance at the sleeping scouts, turned the flashlight on and shone it above them. "Look."

Violet and Klaus looked, and saw that there was a hole in the ceiling, big enough for a person to crawl through. The last wisps of smoke from the fire were floating up into the hole. "A chimney," Klaus murmured. "I was wondering why the fire didn't fill the cave with smoke."

"The official name is Vertical Flame Diversion," the scout whispered. "It serves as a chimney and as a secret passageway. It runs from this cave to the Valley of Four Drafts. If we climb up there, we can reach headquarters within hours, instead of hiking all the way up the mountain. Years ago, there was a metal pole that ran down the center of the hole, so people could slide down and hide in this cave in case of an emergency. The pole is gone now, but there should be carved toeholds in the sides to climb all the way up." He shone the flashlight on the cave wall, and sure enough, the Baudelaires could see two rows of small carved holes, perfect for sticking one's feet and hands into.

"How do you know all this?" Violet asked.

The scout looked at her for a moment, and it seemed to the Baudelaires that he was smiling behind his mask. "I read it," he said, "in a book called *Remarkable Phenomena of the Mortmain Mountains.*"

"That sounds familiar," Klaus said.

"It should," the scout replied. "I borrowed it from Dr. Montgomery's library."

Dr. Montgomery was one of the Baudelaires' first guardians, and at the mention of his name Violet and Klaus found they had several more questions they wanted to ask.

"When—" Violet started.

"Why—" Klaus started.

"Carm—" Another voice startled the Baudelaires and the scout—the voice of Bruce, waking up halfway at the sound of the conversation. All three children froze for a moment, as Bruce turned over on his blanket, and with a long sigh, went back to sleep.

"We'll talk when we reach the headquarters," the scout whispered. "The Vertical Flame Diversion is very echoey, so we'll have to be absolutely silent as we climb, or the echoing noise will alert Bruce and the Snow Scouts. It'll be very dark inside, so you'll have to feel against the wall for the footholds, and the air will be smoky, but if you keep your masks on they'll filter the air and make it easier to breathe. I'll go first and lead the way. Are you ready?"

Violet and Klaus turned toward one another. Even though they could not see each other's faces through the masks, both siblings knew that they were not at all ready. Following a complete stranger into a secret passageway through the center of the mountains, toward a headquarters they could not even be sure existed, did not seem like a very safe thing to do. The last time they had agreed to take a risky journey, their baby sister had been snatched away from them. What would happen this time, when they were all alone with a mysterious masked figure in a dark and smoky hole?

"I know it must be hard to trust me, Baudelaires," said the sweatered scout, "after so many people have done you wrong."

"Can you give us a reason to trust you?" Violet said.

The scout looked down for a moment, and then turned his mask to face both Baudelaires. "One of you mentioned the word 'xenial,'" he said, "when you were talking with Bruce about that silly pledge. 'Xenial' is a word which refers to the giving of gifts to a stranger."

"He's right," Klaus murmured to his sister.

"I know that having a good vocabulary doesn't guarantee that I'm a good person," the boy said. "But it does mean I've read a great deal. And in my experience, well-read people are less likely to be evil."

Violet and Klaus looked at one another through their masks. Neither of them were entirely convinced by what the masked scout had said. There are, of course, plenty of evil people who have read a great many books, and plenty of very kind people who seem to have found some other method of spending their time. But the Baudelaires knew that there was a kind of truth to the boy's statement, and they had to admit that they preferred to take their chances with a stranger who knew what the word "xenial" meant, rather than exiting the cave and trying to find the headquarters all by themselves. So the siblings turned back to the scout, nodded their masks, and followed him to the footholds in the wall, making sure they still had all the items from the caravan with them. The footholds were surprisingly easy to use, and in a short time the Baudelaires were following the mysterious scout into the dark and smoky entrance of the passageway.

The Vertical Flame Diversion that con-nected the Mortmain Mountain headquarters to this particular Volunteer Feline Detectives cave was once one of the most heavily guarded secrets in the world. Anyone who wanted to use it had to correctly answer a series of questions concerning the force of gravity, the habits of carnivorous beasts, and the central themes of Russian novels, so very few people even knew the passageway's exact whereabouts. Until the two Baudelaires' journey, the passageway had not been used for many years, ever since one of my comrades removed the pole in order to use it in the construction of a submarine. So it would be accurate to say that the Vertical Flame Diversion was a road less traveled—even less traveled than the path through the Mortmain Mountains on which this book began.

While the elder Baudelaires had a very good reason to be on the road less traveled, as they were in a great hurry to reach the headquarters and rescue their sister from the clutches of Count Olaf, there is no reason whatsoever why you should be on the road less traveled and choose to read the rest of this woeful chapter, which describes their dark and smoky journey.

The ashen air from the Snow Scouts' fire was difficult to breathe, even through the masks, and Violet and Klaus had to struggle not to cough, knowing that the coughing sound would echo down the passageway and wake up Bruce, but there is no reason for you to struggle through my dismal description of this problem. A number of spiders had noticed the footholds were not being used lately, and had moved in and converted them into spider condominiums, but you are under no obligation to read what happens when spiders are suddenly woken up by the sudden appearance of a climbing foot in their new homes. And as the Baudelaires followed the scout farther and farther up, the strong freezing winds from the top of the mountain would rush through the passageway, and all three youngsters would cling to the footholds with their very lives, hoping that the wind would not blow them back down to the cave floor, but although the Baudelaires found it necessary to keep climbing through the rest of the dark day so they could reach the headquarters as quickly as possible, and I find it necessary to finish describing it, so my account of the Baudelaire case is as accurate and as complete as possible, it is not necessary for you to finish reading the rest of this chapter, so you can be as miserable as possible. My description of the Baudelaires' journey up through the road less traveled begins on the next page, but I beg you not to travel along with them. Instead, you may take a page from Bruce's book, and skip ahead to Chapter Six, and find my report on Sunny Baudelaire's tribulations—a word which here means "opportunities to eavesdrop while cooking for a theater troupe"—with Count Olaf, or you may skip ahead to Chapter Seven, when the elder Baudelaires arrive at the site of the V.F.D. headquarters and unmask the stranger who led them there, or you may take the road very frequently traveled and skip away from this book altogether, and find something better to do with your time besides finishing this unhappy tale and becoming a weary, weeping, and well-read person.

The Baudelaires' journey up the Vertical Flame Diversion was so dark and treacherous that it is not enough to write "The Baudelaires' journey up the Vertical Flame Diversion was so dark and treacherous that it is not enough to write 'The Baudelaires' journey up the Vertical Flame Diversion was so dark and treacherous that it is not enough to write "The Baudelaires' journey up the Vertical Flame Diversion was so dark and treacherous that it is not enough to write 'The Baudelaires' journey up the Vertical Flame Diversion was so dark and treacherous that it is not enough to write "*My dear sister,*
I am taking a great risk in hiding a letter to you inside one of my books, but I am certain that even the most melancholy and well-read people in the world have found my account of the lives of the three Baudelaire children even more wretched than I had promised, and so this book

will stay on the shelves of libraries, utterly ignored, waiting for you to open it and find this message. As an additional precaution, I placed a warning that the rest of this chapter contains a description of the Baudelaires' miserable journey up the Vertical Flame Diversion, so anyone who has the courage to read such a description is probably brave enough to read my letter to you.

I have at last learned the whereabouts of the evidence that will exonerate me, a phrase which here means "prove to the authorities that it is Count Olaf, and not me, who has started so many fires." Your suggestion, so many years ago at that picnic, that a tea set would be a handy place to hide anything important and small in the event of a dark day, has turned out to be correct. (Incidentally, your other picnic suggestion, that a simple combination of sliced mango, black beans, and chopped celery mixed with black pepper, lime juice, and olive oil would make a delicious chilled salad also turned out to be correct.)

I am on my way now to the Valley of Four Drafts, in order to continue my research on the Baudelaire case. I hope also to retrieve the aforementioned evidence at last. It is too late to restore my happiness, of course, but at least I can clear my name. From the site of V.F.D. headquarters, I will head straight for the Hotel Denouement. I should arrive by—well, it wouldn't be wise to type the date, but it should be easy for you to remember Beatrice's birthday. Meet me at the hotel. Try to get us a room without ugly curtains.

With all due respect,

Lemony Snicket

P.S. If you substitute the chopped celery with hearts of palm, it is equally delicious.

In the very early hours of the morning, while the two elder Baudelaires struggled to find their footing as they climbed up the Vertical Flame Diversion—and I sincerely hope that you did not read the description of that journey—the youngest Baudelaire found herself struggling with a different sort of footing altogether. Sunny had not enjoyed the long, cold night on Mount Fraught. If you have ever slept in a covered casserole dish on the highest peak of a mountain range, then you know that it is an uncomfortable place to lay one's head, even if you find a dishtowel inside it that can serve as a blanket. All night long, the chilly mountain winds blew through the tiny holes inside the top of the cover, making it so cold inside the dish that Sunny's enormous teeth chattered all night, giving her tiny cuts on her lips and making such a loud noise that it was impossible to sleep. Finally, when the first rays of the morning sun shone through the holes and made it warm enough to doze, Count Olaf left his tent and kicked open the cover of the dish to begin ordering Sunny around. "Wake up, you dentist's nightmare!" he cried. Sunny opened one exhausted eye and found herself staring at the villain's footing, particularly the tattoo on Olaf's left ankle, a sight that was enough to make her wish her eyes were still closed.

Tattooed on Olaf's ankle was the image of an eye, and it seemed to Sunny that this eye had been watching the Baudelaires throughout all of their troubles, from the day on Briny Beach when they learned of the terrible fire that destroyed their home. Time after time, Count Olaf had tried to hide this eye so the authorities would not recognize him, so the children were always uncovering it from behind his ridiculous disguises, and the Baudelaires had begun seeing the eye in other places, such as at the office of an evil hypnotist, on the side of a carnival tent, on Esmé Squalor's purse, and on a necklace owned by a mysterious fortune-teller. It was almost as if this eye had replaced the eyes of their parents, but instead of keeping watch over the children and making sure that they were safe from harm, this eye merely gave them a blank stare, as if it did not care about the children's troubles, or could do nothing about them. If you looked very closely, you could find the letters V.F.D. half-hidden in the eye, and this reminded Sunny of all the sinister secrets that surrounded the three siblings, and how far they were from understanding the web of mystery in which they found themselves. But it is hard to think about mysteries and secrets first thing in the morning, particularly if someone is yelling at you, and Sunny turned her attention to what her captor was saying.

"You'll be doing all the cooking and cleaning for us, orphan," Count Olaf said, "and you can start by making us breakfast. We have a big day ahead of us, and a good breakfast will give me and my troupe the energy we need to perform unspeakable crimes."

"Plakna?" Sunny asked, which meant "How am I supposed to cook breakfast on the top of a freezing mountain?" but Count Olaf just gave her a nasty smile.

"Too bad your brain isn't as big as your teeth, you little monkey," he said. "You're talking nonsense, as usual."

Sunny sighed, frustrated that there was no one on top of the Mortmain Mountains who understood what she was trying to say. "Translo," she said, which meant "Just because you don't understand something doesn't mean that it's nonsense."

"There you go, babbling again," Olaf said,

and tossed Sunny the car keys. "Get the groceries out of the trunk of the car and get to work."

Sunny suddenly thought of something that might cheer her up a little bit. "Sneakitawc," she said, which was her way of saying "Of course, because you don't understand me, I can say anything I want to you, and you'll have no idea what I'm talking about."

"I'm getting quite tired of your ridiculous speech impediment," Count Olaf said.

"Brummel," Sunny said, which meant "In my opinion, you desperately need a bath, and your clothing is a shambles."

"Be quiet this instant," Olaf ordered.

"Busheney," Sunny said, which meant something along the lines of, "You're an evil man with no concern whatsoever for other people."

"Shut up!" Count Olaf roared. "Shut up and get cooking!"

Sunny got out of the casserole dish and stood up, looking down at the snowy ground so the villain would not see she was smiling. It is not nice to tease people, of course, but the youngest Baudelaire felt that it was all right to enjoy a joke at the expense of such a murderous and evil man, and she walked to Olaf's car with a spring in her step, a phrase which here means "in a surprisingly cheerful manner considering she was in the clutches of a ruthless villain on top of a mountain so cold that even the nearby waterfall was frozen solid."

But when Sunny Baudelaire opened the trunk of the car her smile faded. Under normal circumstances, it is not safe to keep groceries in the trunk of a car for an extended period of time, because some foods will spoil without being refrigerated. But Sunny saw that the temperatures of the Mortmain Mountains had caused the groceries to become over-refrigerated. A thin layer of frost covered every item, and Sunny had to crawl inside and wipe the frost off with her bare hands to see what she might make for the troupe. There was a variety of well-chilled food that Olaf had stolen from the carnival, but none of it seemed like the makings of a good breakfast. There was a bag of coffee beans beneath a harpoon gun and a frozen hunk of spinach, but there was no way to grind the beans into tiny pieces to make coffee. Near a picnic basket and a large bag of mushrooms was a jug of orange juice, but it had been close to one of the bullet holes in the trunk, and so had frozen completely solid in the cold. And after Sunny moved aside three chunks of cold cheese, a large can of water chestnuts, and an eggplant as big as herself, she finally found a small jar of boysenberry jam, and a loaf of bread she could use to make toast, although it was so cold it felt more like a log than a breakfast ingredient.

"Wake up!" Sunny peeked out of the trunk and saw Count Olaf calling through the door of one of the tents she had assembled. "Wake up and get dressed for breakfast!"

"Can't we sleep ten minutes more?" asked the whiny voice of the hook-handed man. "I was having a lovely dream about sneezing without covering my nose and mouth, and giving everybody germs."

"Absolutely not!" Olaf replied. "I have lots of work for you to do."

"But Olaf," said Esmé Squalor, emerging from the tent she had shared with Count Olaf. Her hair was in curlers and she was wearing a long robe and a pair of fuzzy slippers. "I need a little while to choose what I'm going to wear. It's not in to burn down a headquarters without wearing a fashionable outfit."

Sunny gasped in the trunk. She had known that Olaf was eager to reach the V.F.D. headquarters as soon as possible, in order to get his hands on the rest of some crucial evidence, but it had not occurred to her that he would combine this evidence-grabbing with his usual pyromania, a word which here means "a love of fire, usually the product of a deranged mind."

"I can't imagine why you need all this time,"

was Count Olaf's grumpy reply to his girlfriend. "After all, I wear the same outfit for weeks at a time, except when I'm in disguise, and I look almost unbearably handsome. Well, I suppose you have a few minutes before breakfast is ready. Slow service is one of the disadvantages of having infants for slaves." Olaf strode over to the car and peered in at Sunny, who was still clutching the loaf of bread.

"Hurry up, bigmouth," he growled at Sunny. "I need a nice hot meal to take the chill out of the morning."

"Unfeasi!" Sunny cried. By "Unfeasi" she meant "To make a hot meal without any electricity, I'd need a fire, and expecting a baby to start a fire all by herself on top of a snowy mountain is cruelly impossible and impossibly cruel," but Olaf merely frowned.

"Your baby talk is really beginning to annoy me," he said.

"Hygiene," Sunny said, to make herself feel

better. She meant something along the lines of, "Additionally, you ought to be ashamed of yourself for wearing the same outfit for weeks at a time without washing," but Olaf merely scowled at her and walked back into his tent.

Sunny looked at the cold ingredients and tried to think. Even if she had been old enough to start a fire by herself, Sunny had been nervous around flames since the fire that had destroyed the Baudelaire mansion. But as she thought of the fire that destroyed her own home, she remembered something her mother had told her once. They had both been busy in the kitchen—Sunny's mother was busy preparing for a fancy luncheon, and Sunny was busy dropping a fork on the floor over and over again to see what sort of sound it made. The luncheon was due to start any minute, and Sunny's mother was quickly mixing up a salad of sliced mango, black beans, and chopped celery mixed with black pepper, lime juice, and olive oil.

"This isn't a very complicated recipe, Sunny," her mother had said, "but if I arrange the salad very nicely on fancy plates, people will think I've been cooking all day. Often, when cooking, the presentation of the food can be as important as the food itself." Thinking of what her mother had said, she opened the picnic basket in Olaf's trunk and found that it contained a set of elegant plates, each emblazoned with the familiar eye insignia, and a small tea set. Then she rolled up her sleeves—an expression which here means "focused very hard on the task at hand, but did not actually roll up her sleeves, because it was very cold on the highest peak of the Mortmain Mountains"—and got to work as Count Olaf and his comrades started their day.

"I'll use these blankets for a tablecloth," Sunny heard Olaf say in the tent, over the sound her own teeth were making.

"Good idea," she heard Esmé reply. "It's very in to dine *al fresco*."

"What does that mean?" Olaf asked.

"It means 'outside,' of course," Esmé explained. "It's fashionable to eat your meals in the fresh air."

"I knew what it meant," Count Olaf replied. "I was just testing you."

"Hey boss," Hugo called from the next tent. "Colette won't share the dental floss."

"There's no reason to use dental floss," Count Olaf said, "unless you're trying to strangle someone with a very weak neck."

"Kevin, would you do me a favor?" the hook-handed man asked, as Sunny struggled to open the jug of juice. "Will you help me comb my hair? These hooks can make it difficult sometimes."

"I'm jealous of your hooks," Kevin replied. "Having no hands is better than having two equally strong hands."

"Don't be ridiculous," one of the white-faced women replied. "Having a white face is worse than both of your situations."

"But you have a white face because you put makeup on," Colette said, as Sunny climbed back out of the trunk and knelt down in the snow. "You're putting powder on your face right now."

"Must you bicker every single morning?" Count Olaf asked, and stomped back out of his tent carrying a blanket covered in images of eyes. "Somebody take this blanket and set the table over there on that flat rock."

Hugo walked out of the tent and smiled at his new boss. "I'd be happy to," he said.

Esmé stepped outside, having changed into a bright red snowsuit, and put her arm around Olaf. "Fold the blanket into a large triangle," she said to Hugo. "That's the in way to do it."

"Yes ma'am," Hugo said, "and, if you don't mind my saying so, that's a very handsome snowsuit you are wearing."

The villainous girlfriend turned all the way around to show off her outfit from every angle. Sunny looked up from her cooking and noticed that the letter B was sewn onto the back of it, along with the eye insignia. "I'm glad you like it, Hugo," Esmé said. "It's stolen."

Count Olaf glanced at Sunny and quickly stepped in front of his girlfriend. "What are you staring at, toothy?" he asked. "Are you done making breakfast?"

"Almost," Sunny replied.

"That infant never makes any sense," Hugo said. "No wonder she fooled us into thinking she was a carnival freak."

Sunny sighed, but no one heard her over the scornful laughter of Olaf's troupe. One by one, the villain's wretched employees emerged from the tent and strolled over to the flat rock where Hugo was laying out the blanket. One of the white-faced women glanced at Sunny and gave her a small smile, but nobody offered to help her finish with the breakfast preparations, or even to set the table with the eye-patterned dishes. Instead, they gathered around the rock talking and laughing until Sunny carefully carried the breakfast over to them, arranged on a

THE SLIPPERY SLOPE

large eye-shaped tray that she'd found in the bottom of the picnic basket. Although she was still frightened to be in Olaf's clutches and worried about her siblings, Sunny could not help but be a little proud as Count Olaf and his comrades looked at the meal she had prepared.

Sunny had kept in mind what her mother had said about presentation being as important as the food itself, and managed to put together a lovely breakfast despite the difficult circumstances. First, she had opened the jug of frozen orange juice and used a small spoon to chip away at the ice until she had a large heap of juice shavings, which she arranged into tiny piles on each plate to make orange granita, a cold and delicious concoction that is often served at fancy dinner parties and masked balls. Then, Sunny had rinsed her mouth out with melted snow so it would be as clean as possible, and chopped some of the coffee beans with her teeth. She placed a bit of the ground coffee inside each cup and combined it with more snow she had melted in her own hands to make iced coffee, a delicious beverage I first enjoyed when visiting Thailand to interview a taxi driver. Meanwhile, the youngest Baudelaire had put the chilled bread underneath her shirt to warm it up, and when it was warm enough to eat she put one slice on each plate, and using a small spoon, spread some boysenberry jam on each piece of bread. She did her best to spread the jam in the shape of an eye, to please the villains who would be eating it, and as a finishing touch she found a bouquet of ivy, which Count Olaf had given his girlfriend not so long ago, and placed it in the small pitcher of the tea set used for cream. There was no cream, but the ivy would help the presentation of the food by serving as a centerpiece, a word which here means "a decoration placed in the middle of a table, often used to distract people from the food." Of course, orange granita and iced coffee are not often served at *al fresco* breakfasts on cold mountain peaks, and bread with jam is more traditionally prepared as toast, but without a source of heat or any other cooking equipment, Sunny had done the best she could, and she hoped that Olaf and his troupe might appreciate her efforts.

"Caffefredde, sorbet, toast tartar," she announced.

"What is this?" Count Olaf said suspiciously, peering into his coffee cup. "It looks like coffee, but it's freezing cold!"

"And what is this orange stuff?" Esmé asked suspiciously. "I want fashionable, in food, not a handful of ice!"

Colette picked up a piece of the bread and stared at it suspiciously. "This toast feels raw," she said. "Is it safe to eat raw toast?"

"Of course not," Hugo said. "I bet that baby is trying to poison us."

"Actually, the coffee isn't bad," one of the white-faced women said, "even if it is a little bitter. Could someone pass the sugar, please?"

"*Sugar?*" shrieked Count Olaf, erupting in

anger. He stood up, grabbed one end of the blanket, and pulled as hard as he could, scattering all of Sunny's hard work. Food, beverages, and dishes fell everywhere, and Sunny had to duck to avoid getting hit on the head with a flying fork. "All the sugar in the world couldn't save this terrible breakfast!" he roared, and then leaned down so that his shiny, shiny eyes stared right into Sunny's. "I told you to make a nice, hot breakfast, and you gave me cold, disgusting nonsense!" he said, his smelly breath making a cloud in the chilly air. "Don't you see how high up we are, you sabertoothed papoose? If I threw you off Mount Fraught, you'd never survive!"

"Olaf!" Esmé said. "I'm surprised at you! Surely you remember that we'll never get the Baudelaire fortune if we toss Sunny off the mountain. We have to keep Sunny alive for the greater good."

"Yes, yes," Count Olaf said. "I remember. I'm not going to throw the orphan off the mountain. I just wanted to terrify her." He gave Sunny a cruel smirk, and then turned to the hook-handed man. "Walk over to that frozen water-fall," he said, "and crack a hole in the ice with your hook. The stream is full of Stricken Salmon. Catch enough for all of us, and we'll have the baby prepare us a proper meal."

"Good idea, Olaf," the hook-handed man said, standing up and walking toward the icy slope. "You're as smart as you are intelligent."

"Sakesushi," Sunny said quietly, which meant "I don't think you'll enjoy salmon if it's not cooked."

"Stop your baby talk and wash these dishes," Olaf ordered. "They're covered in lousy food."

"You know, Olaf," said the white-faced woman who had asked for sugar, "it's none of my business, but we might put someone else in charge of cooking. It was probably difficult for a baby to prepare a hot breakfast without a fire."

"But there is a fire," said a deep, low voice, and everyone turned around to see who had arrived.

Having an aura of menace is like having a pet weasel, because you rarely meet someone who has one, and when you do it makes you want to hide under the coffee table. An aura of menace is simply a distinct feeling of evil that accompanies the arrival of certain people, and very few individuals are evil enough to produce an aura of menace that is very strong. Count Olaf, for example, had an aura of menace that the three Baudelaires had felt the moment they met him, but a number of other people never seemed to sense that a villain was in their midst, even when Olaf was standing right next to them with an evil gleam in his eye. But when two visitors arrived at the highest peak of the Mortmain Mountains, their aura of menace was unmistakable. Sunny gasped when she saw them. Esmé Squalor shuddered in her snowsuit. The members of Olaf's troupe—all except the hook-handed man, who was busy fishing for salmon and so was lucky enough to miss the visitors' arrival—gazed down at the snowy ground rather than take a further look at them. Count Olaf himself looked a bit nervous as the man, the woman, and their aura of menace drew closer and closer. And even I, after all this time, can feel their aura of menace so strongly, just by writing about these two people, that I dare not say their names, and will instead refer to them the way everyone who dares refer to them refers to them, as "the man with a beard, but no hair" and "the woman with hair, but no beard."

"It's good to see you, Olaf," continued the deep voice, and Sunny realized that the voice belonged to the sinister-looking woman. She was dressed in a suit made of a strange blue fabric that was very shiny, decorated with two large pads, one on each shoulder. She was dragging a wooden toboggan—a word which here means "a sled big enough to hold several people," which made an eerie scraping sound against the cold ground. "I was worried that the authorities might have captured you."

"You look well," said the man with a beard

but no hair. He was dressed identically to the woman with hair but no beard, but his voice was very hoarse, as if he had been screaming for hours and could hardly talk. "It's been a long time since we've laid eyes on one another." The man gave Olaf a grin that made it seem even colder on the mountain peak, and then stopped and helped the woman lean the toboggan against the rock where Sunny had served breakfast. The youngest Baudelaire saw that the toboggan was painted with the familiar eye insignia, and had a few long leather straps, presumably used for steering.

Count Olaf coughed lightly into his hand, which is something people often do when they cannot think of what to say. "Hello," he said, a bit nervously. "Did I hear you say something about a fire?"

The man with a beard but no hair and the woman with hair but no beard looked at one another and shared a laugh that made Sunny cover her ears with her hands. "Haven't you noticed," the woman said, "that there are no snow gnats around?"

"We had noticed that," Esmé said. "I thought maybe snow gnats were no longer in."

"Don't be ridiculous, Esmé," said the man with a beard but no hair. He reached out and kissed Esmé's hand, which Sunny could see was trembling. "The gnats aren't around because they can smell the smoke."

"I don't smell anything," said Hugo.

"Well, if you were a tiny insect, you'd smell something," replied the woman with hair but no beard. "If you were a snow gnat, you'd smell the smoke from the V.F.D. headquarters."

"We did you a favor, Olaf," the man said. "We burned the entire place down."

"No!" Sunny cried, before she could stop herself. By "No!" she meant "I certainly hope that isn't true, because my siblings and I hoped to reach V.F.D. headquarters, solve the mysteries that surround us, and perhaps find one of our parents," but she had not planned to say it out loud. The two visitors looked down at the young-est Baudelaire, casting their aura of menace in her direction.

"What is that?" asked the man with a beard but no hair.

"That's the youngest Baudelaire," replied Esmé. "We've eliminated the other two, but we're keeping this one around to do our bidding until we can finally steal the fortune."

The woman with hair but no beard nodded. "Infant servants are so troublesome," she said. "I had an infant servant once—a long time ago, before the schism."

"Before the schism?" Olaf said, and Sunny wished Klaus were with her, because the baby did not know what the word "schism" meant. "That *is* a long time ago. That infant must be all grown up by now."

"Not necessarily," the woman said, and laughed again, while her companion leaned down to gaze at Sunny. Sunny could not bear to look into the eyes of the man with a beard but no hair, and instead looked down at his shiny shoes.

"So this is Sunny Baudelaire," he said in his strange, hoarse voice. "Well, well, well. I've heard so much about this little orphan. She's caused almost as many problems as her parents did." He stood up again and looked around at Olaf and his troupe. "But we know how to solve problems, don't we? Fire can solve any problem in the world."

He began to laugh, and the woman with hair but no beard laughed along with him. Nervously, Count Olaf began to laugh, too, and then glared at his troupe until they laughed along with him, and Sunny found herself surrounded by tall, laughing villains. "Oh, it was wonderful," said the woman with hair but no beard. "First we burned down the kitchen. Then we burned down the dining room. Then we burned down the parlor, and then the disguise center, the movie room, and the stables. Then we moved on to the gymnasium and the training center, and the garage and all six of the laboratories. We burned down the dormitories and schoolrooms, the lounge, the theater, and the music room, as well as the museum and the ice cream shop. Then we burned down the rehearsal studios and the testing centers and the swimming pool, which was very hard to burn down. Then we burned down all the bathrooms, and then finally, we burned down the V.F.D. library last night. That was my favorite part—books and books and books, all turned to ashes so no one could read them. You should have been there, Olaf! Every morning we lit fires and every evening we celebrated with a bottle of wine and some finger puppets. We've been wearing these fireproof suits for almost a month. It's been a marvelous time."

"Why did you burn it down gradually?" Count Olaf asked. "Whenever I burn something down, I do it all at once."

"We couldn't have burned down the entire headquarters at once," said the man with a beard but no hair. "Someone would have spotted us.

Remember, where there's smoke there's fire."

"But if you burned the headquarters down room by room," Esmé said, "didn't all of the volunteers escape?"

"They were gone already," said the man, and scratched his head where his hair might have been. "The entire headquarters were deserted. It was as if they knew we were coming. Oh well, you can't win them all."

"Maybe we'll find some of them when we burn down the carnival," said the woman, in her deep, deep voice.

"Carnival?" Olaf asked nervously.

"Yes," the woman said, and scratched the place where her beard would have been, if she had one. "There's an important piece of evidence that V.F.D. has hidden in a figurine sold at Caligari Carnival, so we need to go burn it down."

"I burned it down already," Count Olaf said.

"The whole place?" the woman said in surprise.

"The whole place," Olaf said, giving her a nervous smile.

"Congratulations," she said, in a deep purr. "You're better than I thought, Olaf."

Count Olaf looked relieved, as if he had not been sure whether the woman was going to compliment him or kick him. "Well, it's all for the greater good," he said.

"As a reward," the woman said, "I have a gift for you, Olaf." Sunny watched as the woman reached into the pocket of her shiny suit and drew out a stack of paper, tied together with thick rope. The paper looked very old and worn, as if it had been passed around to a variety of different people, hidden in a number of secret compartments, and perhaps even divided into different piles, driven around a city in horse-drawn carriages, and then put back together at midnight in the back room of a bookstore disguised as a café disguised as a sporting goods store. Count Olaf's eyes grew very wide and very shiny, and he reached his filthy hands toward it as if it were the Baudelaire fortune itself.

"The Snicket file!" he said, in a hushed whisper.

"It's all here," the woman said. "Every chart, every map and every photograph from the only file that could put us all in jail."

"It's complete except for page thirteen, of course," the man said. "We understand that the Baudelaires managed to steal that page from Heimlich Hospital."

The two visitors glared down at Sunny Baudelaire, who couldn't help whimpering in fear. "Surchmi," she said. She meant something along the lines of, "I don't have it—my siblings do," but she did not need a translator.

"The older orphans have it," Olaf said, "but I'm fairly certain they're dead."

"Then all of our problems have gone up in smoke," said the woman with hair but no beard.

Count Olaf grabbed the file and held it to his chest as if it were a newborn baby, although he was not the sort of person to treat a newborn baby very kindly. "This is the most wonderful gift in the world," he said. "I'm going to go read it right now."

"We'll all read it together," said the woman with hair but no beard. "It contains secrets we all ought to know."

"But first," said the man with a beard but no hair, "I have a gift for your girlfriend, Olaf."

"For me?" Esmé asked.

"I found these in one of the rooms of head-quarters," the man said. "I've never seen one before, but it has been quite some time since I was a volunteer." With a sly smile, he reached into his pocket and took out a small green tube.

"What's that?" Esmé asked.

"I think it's a cigarette," the man said.

"A cigarette!" Esmé said, with a smile as big as Olaf's. "How in!"

"I thought you'd enjoy them," the man said. "Here, try it. I happen to have quite a few matches right here."

The man with a beard but no hair struck a

match, lit the end of the green tube, and offered it to the wicked girlfriend, who grabbed it and held it to her mouth. A bitter smell, like that of burning vegetables, filled the air, and Esmé Squalor began to cough.

"What's the matter?" asked the woman in her deep voice. "I thought you liked things that are in."

"I do," Esmé said, and then coughed quite a bit more. Sunny was reminded of Mr. Poe, who was always coughing into a handkerchief, as Esmé coughed and coughed and finally dropped the green tube to the ground where it spewed out a dark green smoke. "I love cigarettes," she explained to the man with a beard but no hair, "but I prefer to smoke them with a long holder because I don't like the smell or taste and because they're very bad for you."

"Never mind that now," Count Olaf said impatiently. "Let's go into my tent and read the file." He started to walk toward the tent but stopped and glared at his comrades, who were beginning to follow him. "The rest of you stay out here," he said. "There are secrets in this file that I do not want you to know."

The two sinister visitors began to laugh, and followed Count Olaf and Esmé into the tent, closing the flap behind them. Sunny stood with Hugo, Colette, Kevin, and the two white-faced women and stared after them in silence, waiting for the aura of menace to disappear.

"Who were those people?" asked the hook-handed man, and everyone turned to see that he had returned from his fishing expedition. Four salmon hung from each of his hooks, dripping with the waters of the Stricken Stream.

"I don't know," said one of the white-faced women, "but they made me very nervous."

"If they're friends of Count Olaf's," Kevin said, "how bad could they be?"

The members of the troupe looked at one another, but no one answered the ambidextrous person's question. "What did that man mean when he said 'Where there's smoke there's fire'?" Hugo asked.

"I don't know," Colette said. A chilly wind blew, and Sunny watched her contort her body in the breeze until it looked almost as curvy as the smoke from the green tube Esmé had dropped.

"Forget those questions," the hook-handed man said. "My question is, how are you going to prepare this salmon, orphan?"

Olaf's henchman was looking down at Sunny, but the youngest Baudelaire did not answer for a moment. Sunny was thinking, and her siblings would have been proud of her for the way she was thinking. Klaus would have been proud, because she was thinking about the phrase "Where there's smoke there's fire," and what it might mean. And Violet would have been proud, because she was thinking about the salmon that the hook-handed man was holding, and what she might invent that would help her.

Sunny stared at the hook-handed man and thought as hard as she could, and she felt almost as if both siblings were with her, Klaus helping her think about a phrase and Violet helping her think about an invention.

"Answer me, baby," the hook-handed man growled. "What are you going to make for us out of this salmon?"

"Lox!" Sunny said, but it was as if all three of the Baudelaires had answered the question.

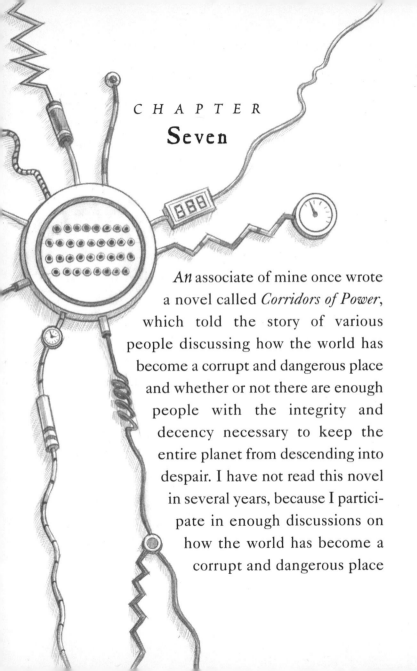

An associate of mine once wrote
a novel called *Corridors of Power*,
which told the story of various
people discussing how the world has
become a corrupt and dangerous place
and whether or not there are enough
people with the integrity and
decency necessary to keep the
entire planet from descending into
despair. I have not read this novel
in several years, because I participate in enough discussions on
how the world has become a
corrupt and dangerous place

and whether or not there are enough people with the integrity and decency necessary to keep the entire planet from descending into despair without reading about it in my leisure time, but nevertheless the phrase "corridors of power" has come to mean the hushed and often secret places where important matters are discussed. Whether or not they are actual corridors, the corridors of power tend to feel quiet and mysterious. If you have ever walked inside an important building, such as the main branch of a library or the office of a dentist who has agreed to disguise your teeth, then you may have experienced this feeling that accompanies the corridors of power, and Violet and Klaus Baudelaire experienced it as they reached the end of the Vertical Flame Diversion, and followed the mysterious sweatered scout as he climbed out of the secret passageway. Even through their masks, the two siblings could sense that they were in an important place, even though it was nothing more than a dim, curved hallway with a small grate on the ceiling where the morning light was shining through.

"That's where the smoke escapes from the Snow Scouts' fire," whispered the mysterious scout, pointing up at the ceiling. "That leads to the very center of the Valley of Four Drafts, so the smoke is scattered to the four winds. V.F.D. doesn't want anyone to see the smoke."

"Where there's smoke," Violet said, "there's fire."

"Exactly," the scout said. "Anyone who saw smoke coming from this high up in the mountains might become suspicious and investigate. In fact, I found a device that works exactly according to this principle." He reached into his backpack and drew out a small rectangular box filled with small green tubes, exactly like the one that Sunny had seen the man with a beard but no hair give to Esmé Squalor.

"No thank you," Violet said. "I don't smoke."

"I don't, either," the scout said, "but these aren't cigarettes. These are Verdant Flammable

Devices. Verdant means 'green,' so when you light one, it gives out a dark green smoke, so another volunteer will know where you are."

Klaus took the box from the scout and squinted at it in the dim light. "I've seen a box like this before," he said, "in my father's desk, when I was looking for a letter opener. I remember thinking it was strange to find them, because he didn't smoke."

"He must have been hiding them," Violet said. "Why was he keeping them a secret?"

"The entire organization is a secret," the scout said. "It was very difficult for me to learn the secret location of the headquarters."

"It was difficult for us, too," Klaus said. "We found it in a coded map."

"I had to draw my own map," the scout said, and reached into a pocket in his sweater. He turned on the flashlight, and the two Baudelaires could see he was holding a notebook with a dark purple cover.

"What's that?" Violet asked.

"It's a commonplace book," the scout said. "Whenever I find something that seems important or interesting, I write it down. That way, all my important information is in one place."

"I should start one," Klaus said. "My pockets are bulging with scraps of paper."

"From information I read in Dr. Montgomery's book, and a few others," the scout said, "I managed to draw a map of where to go from here." He opened the purple notebook and flipped a few pages until he reached a small but elegant rendering of the cave, the Vertical Flame Diversion, and the hallway in which they were standing now. "As you can see," he said, running his finger along the hallway, "the passageway branches off in two directions."

"This is a very well-drawn map," Violet said.

"Thank you," the scout replied. "I've been interested in cartography for quite some time. See, if we go to the left, there's a small area used for sled and snowsuit storage, at least according to a newspaper article I found. But if we go right, we'll arrive at the Vernacularly Fastened Door, which should open onto the headquarters' kitchen. We might walk in on the entire organization having breakfast."

The two Baudelaires looked at one another through their masks, and Violet put a hand on her brother's shoulder. They did not dare to say out loud their hope that one of their parents might be just around the corner. "Let's go," Violet whispered.

The scout nodded silently in agreement, and led the Baudelaires down the hallway, which seemed to get colder and colder with every step. By now they were so far from Bruce and the Snow Scouts that there was no need to whisper, but all three children kept quiet as they walked down the dim, curved hallway, hushed by the feeling of the corridors of power. At last they reached a large metal door with a strange device where the doorknob should have been. The device looked a bit like a spider, with curly wires spreading out in all directions, but where the head of the spider might have been was the keyboard of a typewriter. Even in her excitement to see the headquarters, Violet's inventing mind was interested in such a device, and she leaned closer to see what it was.

"Wait," the sweatered scout said, reaching his arm out to stop her. "This is a coded lock. If we don't operate it properly, we won't be able to get into the headquarters."

"How does it work?" Violet said, shivering slightly in the cold.

"I'm not sure," the scout admitted, and took out his commonplace book again. "It's called the Vernacularly Fastened Door, so—"

"So it operates on language," Klaus finished. "Vernacular is a word for 'a local language or dialect.'"

"Of course," Violet said. "See how the wires are curled around the hinges of the door? They're locked in place, unless you type in the right sequence of letters on that keyboard. There are more letters than numbers, so it would be more difficult for someone to guess the combination of the lock."

"That's what I read," the scout confirmed, looking at a page in his notebook. "You're supposed to type in three specific phrases in a row. The phrases change every season, so volunteers need to have a lot of information at their fingertips to use this door. The first is the name of the scientist most widely credited with the discovery of gravity."

"That's easy," Violet said, and typed in S-I-R-I-S-A-A-C-N-E-W-T-O-N, the name of a physicist she had always admired. When she was finished, there was a muted clicking sound from the typewriter keyboard, as if the device was warming up.

"The second is the Latin name for the Volunteer Feline Detectives," the scout said. "I found the answer in *Remarkable Phenomena of the Mortmain Mountains*. It's *Panthera leo*." He leaned forward and typed in P-A-N-T-H-E-R-A-L-E-O. There was a very quiet buzzing sound, and the children saw that the wires near the hinges were shaking very slightly.

"It's beginning to unlock," Violet said. "I hope I get a chance to study this invention."

"Let's get to the headquarters first," Klaus said. "What's the third phrase?"

The scout sighed, and turned a page in the commonplace book. "I'm not sure," he admitted. "Another volunteer told me that it's the central theme of Leo Tolstoy's novel *Anna Karenina*, but I haven't had a chance to read it yet."

Violet knew that her brother was smiling, even though she could not see his face through the mask. She was remembering one summer, very long ago, when Klaus was very young and Sunny was not even conceived. Every summer, the Baudelaires' mother would read a very long book, joking that lifting a large novel was the only exercise she liked to get during the hot months. During the time Violet was thinking of, Mrs. Baudelaire chose *Anna Karenina* for her summer reading, and Klaus would sit on his mother's lap for hours at a time while she read. The middle Baudelaire had not been reading very long, but their mother helped him with the big words and would occasionally stop reading to explain what had happened in the story, and in this way Klaus and his mother read the story of Ms. Karenina, whose boyfriend treats her so poorly that she throws herself under a train. Violet had spent most of that summer studying the laws of thermodynamics and building a miniature helicopter out of an eggbeater and some old copper wiring, but she knew that Klaus must remember the central theme of the book he read on his mother's lap.

"The central theme of *Anna Karenina*," he said, "is that a rural life of moral simplicity, despite its monotony, is the preferable personal narrative to a daring life of impulsive passion, which only leads to tragedy."

"That's a very long theme," the scout said.

"It's a very long book," Klaus replied. "But I can work quickly. My sisters and I once tapped out a long telegram in no time at all."

"Too bad that telegram never arrived," the scout said quietly, but the middle Baudelaire was already pressing the keys on the Vernacularly Fastened Door. As Klaus typed the words "a rural life," a phrase which here means "living in the country," the wires began to curl and uncurl very quickly, like worms on a sidewalk after it has rained, and by the time Klaus was typing "the preferable personal narrative," a phrase which here means "the way to live your life," the entire door was quivering as if it were as nervous as the Baudelaires. Finally, Klaus typed "T-R-A-G-E-D-Y," and the three children stepped back, but instead of opening, the door stopped shaking and the wires stopped moving, and the passageway was dead quiet.

"It's not opening," Violet said. "Maybe that isn't the central theme of Leo Tolstoy's *Anna Karenina*."

"It seemed like it was working until the last word," the scout said.

"Maybe the mechanism is a little stuck," Violet said.

"Or maybe a daring life of impulsive passion only leads to something else," the scout said, and in some cases this mysterious person was right. A daring life of impulsive passion is an expression which refers to people who follow what is in their hearts, and like people who prefer to follow their head, or follow the advice of other people, or follow a mysterious man in a dark blue raincoat, people who lead a daring life of impulsive passion end up doing all sorts of things. For instance, if you ever find yourself reading a book entitled The Bible, you would find the story of Adam and Eve, whose daring life of impulsive passion led to them putting on clothing for the first time in their lives, in order to leave the snake-infested garden where they had been living. Bonnie and Clyde, another famous couple who lived a daring life of impulsive passion, found that it led them to a successful if short career in bank robbery. And in my own case, in the few moments where I have led a daring life of impulsive passion, it has led to all sorts of trouble, from false accusations of arson to a broken cuff link I can never have repaired. But in this case, as the Baudelaires stood at the Vernacularly Fastened Door, hoping to reach the V.F.D. headquarters, rescue their sister, and see if one of their parents was indeed alive, it was not the sweatered scout but the two Baudelaires who were right, because in Leo Tolstoy's *Anna Karenina*, a daring life of impulsive passion leads only to tragedy, as Klaus said, and as Violet said, the mechanism was a little stuck, and after a few seconds, the door swung open with a slow and eerie creak. The children stepped through the door, blinking in the sudden light, and stood frozen in their steps. If you have read this far in the Baudelaires' woeful story, then you will not be surprised to learn that the V.F.D. headquarters in the Valley of Four Drafts in the Mortmain Mountains was no more, but Violet and

Klaus, of course, were not reading their own story. They were in their own story, and this was the part of their story where they were sick with shock at what they saw.

The Vernacularly Fastened Door did not open onto a kitchen, not anymore. When the Baudelaires followed the mysterious scout through the doorway, they found themselves standing in what at first seemed to be a large field, growing a black and ruined harvest in a valley as cold and drafty as its name. But slowly, they saw the charred remains of the grand and impressive building that had stood where the three children were standing. Nearby was a handful of silverware that had survived the blaze, scattered in front of the remnants of a stove, and a refrigerator stood to one side, as if it were guarding the ashen remains of the rest of the kitchen. To one side was a pile of burnt wood that had probably once been a large dining table, with a half-melted candelabra sticking out of the top like a baby tree. Farther away, they could see the mysterious shapes of other objects that had survived the fire—a trombone, the pendulum of a grandfather clock, what looked like a periscope, or perhaps a spyglass, an ice cream scoop, lying forlornly in a pile of ashes encrusted with burnt sugar, and an iron archway emblazoned with the words "V.F.D. Library," but there was nothing beyond the archway but piles and piles of blackened remains. It was a devastating sight, and it made Violet and Klaus feel as if they were all alone in a world that had been completely ruined. The only thing they could see that seemed untouched by the fire was a sheer, white wall, beyond the refrigerator, that rose up as far as two siblings could see. It took the Baudelaires a few moments to realize that it was a frozen waterfall, rising up in a slippery slope toward the source of the Stricken Stream on Mount Fraught, so shiny and white that it made the ruined headquarters look even darker.

"It must have been beautiful," the sweatered scout said, in a quivering voice. He walked toward the waterfall, his feet churning up black dust with every step. "I read that there was a large window," he said, moving his gloved hand in the air as if it were still there. "When it was your turn to cook, you could look out at the waterfall while you were chopping vegetables or simmering a sauce. It was supposed to be very peaceful. And there was a mechanism just outside the window that turned some of the water from the pool into steam. The steam rose up and covered the headquarters, so it couldn't be seen through the blanket of mist."

The Baudelaires walked to where the scout was standing, and looked into the frozen pool at the bottom of the waterfall. The pool branched off into two tributaries, a word which here means "divisions of a river or stream, each twisting off in a different direction past the ruins of the head-quarters, and curving around the Mortmain Mountains until they disappeared from view." Violet and Klaus gazed sadly at the icy swirls of black and gray they had noticed when they were walking alongside the Stricken Stream. "It was ashes," Klaus said quietly. "Ashes from the fire fell into the pool at the bottom of the waterfall, and the stream carried them down the river."

Violet found that it was easier to discuss a small, specific matter than think about her immense disappointment. "But the pool is frozen solid," she said. "The stream couldn't have carried the ashes anywhere."

"It wouldn't have been frozen when it happened," Klaus replied. "The heat from the fire would have thawed the pool."

"It must have been awful to see," the sweatered scout said. Violet and Klaus stood with him, imagining the inferno, a word which here means "enormous fire that destroyed a secret headquarters high in the mountains." They could almost hear the shattering of glass as the windows fell away, and the crackle of the fire as it consumed everything it could. They could almost smell the thick smoke as it floated upward and blackened the sky, and they could almost see the books in the library, falling from the burning shelves and tumbling into ashes. The only thing they could not picture was who might have been at the headquarters when the fire began, running out into the freezing cold to avoid the flames.

"Do you think," Violet said, "any of the volunteers . . ."

"There's no sign that anyone was here," the scout said quickly.

"But how can we know for sure?" Klaus asked. "There could be a survivor someplace right now."

"*Hello?*" Violet called, looking around her at the rubble. "*Hello?*" She found that her eyes were filling with tears, as she called out for the people she knew in her heart were nowhere nearby. The eldest Baudelaire felt as if she had been calling for these people since that terrible day on the beach, and that if she called them enough they might appear before her. She thought of all the times she had called them, back when she lived with her siblings in the Baudelaire mansion.

Sometimes she called them when she wanted them to see something she had invented. Sometimes she called them when she wanted them to know she had arrived home. And sometimes she called them just because she wanted to know where they were. Sometimes Violet just wanted to see them, and feel that she was safe as long as they were around. *"Mother!"* Violet Baudelaire called. *"Father!"*

There was no answer.

"Mom!" Klaus called. *"Dad!"*

The Baudelaires heard nothing but the rush of all four of the valley's drafts, and a long creak as the Vernacularly Fastened Door blew shut. They saw that the door had been made to look just like the side of the mountain, so that they could scarcely see where they had come from, or the way to get back. Now they were truly alone.

"I know we were all hoping to find people at the headquarters," the sweatered scout said gently, "but I don't think anyone is here. I think we're all by ourselves."

"That's *impossible*!" Klaus cried, and Violet could hear that he was crying. He reached through his layers of clothing until he found his pocket, and pulled out page thirteen from the Snicket file, which he had been carrying with him since the Baudelaires had found it at Heimlich Hospital. The page had a photograph of their parents, standing with Jacques Snicket and another man the Baudelaires had been unable to identify, and above the photograph was a sentence Klaus had memorized from reading it so many times. "'Because of the evidence discussed on page nine,'" he recited tearfully, "'experts now suspect that there may in fact be one survivor of the fire, but the survivor's whereabouts are unknown.'" He walked up to the scout and shook the page in his face. "We thought the survivor would be here," he said.

"I think the survivor *is* here," the scout said quietly, and removed his mask to reveal his face at last. "I'm Quigley Quagmire," he said, "I survived the fire that destroyed my home, and I was hoping to find my brother and sister."

CHAPTER Eight

It is one of the peculiar truths of life that people often say things that they know full well are ridiculous. If someone asks you how you are, for example, you might automatically say "Fine, thank you," when in fact you have just failed an examination or been trampled by an ox. A friend might tell you, "I've looked every-where in the world for my keys," when you know that they have actually only looked in a few places in the immediate area. Once I said to a woman I loved very much, "I'm sure that this trouble will end soon, and you and I will spend the rest of our lives together in happiness and bliss," when I actually suspected that things were about to get much worse. And so it was with the two elder Baudelaires, when they stood face-to-face with Quigley Quagmire and found themselves to be saying things they knew were absurd.

"You're dead," Violet said, and took off her mask to make sure she was seeing things clearly. But there was no mistaking Quigley, even though the Baudelaires had never seen him before. He looked so much like Duncan and Isadora that he could only be the third Quagmire triplet.

"You perished in a fire along with your parents," Klaus said, but as he took off his mask he knew this wasn't so. Quigley was even giving the two Baudelaires a small smile that looked exactly like his siblings'.

"No," Quigley said. "I survived, and I've been looking for my siblings ever since."

"But how did you survive?" Violet asked.

"Duncan and Isadora said that the house burned to the ground."

"It did," Quigley said sadly. He looked out at the frozen waterfall and sighed deeply. "I suppose I should start at the beginning. I was in my family's library, studying a map of the Finite Forest, when I heard a shattering of glass, and people shouting. My mother ran into the room and said there was a fire. We tried to go out the front door but the main hall was filled with smoke, so she took me back into the library and lifted a corner of the rug. There was a secret door underneath. She told me to wait down below while she fetched my siblings, and she left me there in the dark. I remember hearing the house falling to pieces above me, and the sound of frantic footsteps, and my siblings screaming." Quigley put his mask down on the ground and looked at the two Baudelaires. "But she never came back," he said. "Nobody came back, and when I tried to open the door, something had fallen on top of it and it wouldn't budge."

"How did you get out?" Klaus asked.

"I walked," Quigley said. "When it became clear that no one was going to rescue me, I felt around in the dark and realized I was in a sort of passageway. There was nowhere else to go, so I started walking. I've never been so frightened in my life, walking alone in some dark passageway my parents had kept secret. I couldn't imagine where it would lead."

The two Baudelaires looked at one another. They were thinking about the secret passageway they had discovered underneath their home, which they had discovered when they were under the care of Esmé Squalor and her husband. "And where did it lead?" Violet said.

"To the house of a herpetologist," Quigley said. "At the end of the passageway was a secret door that opened into an enormous room, made entirely of glass. The room was filled with empty cages, but it was clear that the room had once housed an enormous collection of reptiles."

"We've been there!" Klaus cried in amazement. "That's Uncle Monty's house! He was our guardian until Count Olaf arrived, disguised as—"

"As a lab assistant," Quigley finished. "I know. His suitcase was still there."

"There was a secret passageway under our house, too," Violet said, "but we didn't discover it until we lived with Esmé Squalor."

"There are secrets everywhere," Quigley said. "I think everyone's parents have secrets. You just have to know where to look for them."

"But why would our parents, and yours, have tunnels underneath their homes leading to a fancy apartment building and a herpetologist's home?" Klaus said. "It doesn't make any sense."

Quigley sighed, and put his backpack on the ashen ground, next to his mask. "There's a lot that doesn't make sense," he said. "I was hoping to find the answers here, but now I don't know if I'll ever find them." He took out his purple notebook and opened it to the first page.

"All I can tell you is what I have here in this commonplace book."

Klaus gave Quigley a small smile, and reached into his pockets to retrieve all of the papers he had stored there. "You tell us what you know," he said, "and we'll tell you what we know. Perhaps together we can answer our own questions."

Quigley nodded in agreement, and the three children sat in a circle on what was once the kitchen floor. Quigley opened his backpack and took out a bag of salted almonds, which he passed around. "You must be hungry from the climb up the Vertical Flame Diversion," he said. "I know I am. Let's see, where was I?"

"In the Reptile Room," Violet said, "at the end of the passageway."

"Well, nothing happened for a while," Quigley said. "On the doorstep of the house was a copy of *The Daily Punctilio*, which had an article about the fire. That's how I learned that my parents were dead. I spent days and days there, all by myself. I was so sad, and so scared, and I didn't know what else to do. I suppose I was waiting for the herpetologist to show up for work, and see if he was a friend of my parents and might be of some assistance. The kitchen was filled with food, so I had enough to eat, and every night I slept at the bottom of the stairs, so I could hear if anyone came in."

The Baudelaires nodded sympathetically, and Violet put a comforting hand on Quigley's shoulder. "We were the same way," Violet said, "right when we heard the news about our parents. I scarcely remember what we did and what we said."

"But didn't anyone come looking for you?" Klaus asked.

"*The Daily Punctilio* said that I died in the fire, too," Quigley said. "The article said that my sister and brother were sent off to Prufrock Preparatory School, and that my parents' estate was under the care of the city's sixth most important financial advisor."

"*Esmé Squalor*," Violet and Klaus said simultaneously, a word which here means "in a disgusted voice, and at the exact same time."

"Right," Quigley said, "but I wasn't interested in that part of the story. I was determined to go to the school and find my siblings again. I found an atlas in Dr. Montgomery's library, and studied it until I found Prufrock Preparatory School. It wasn't too far, so I started to gather whatever supplies I could find around his house."

"Didn't you think of calling the authorities?" Klaus asked.

"I guess I wasn't thinking very clearly," Quigley admitted. "All I could think of was finding my siblings."

"Of course," Violet said. "So what happened then?"

"I was interrupted," Quigley said. "Someone walked in just as I was putting the atlas in a totebag I found. It was Jacques Snicket, although I didn't know who he was, of course. But he knew who I was, and was overjoyed that

I was alive after all."

"How did you know you could trust him?" Klaus asked.

"Well, he knew about the secret passageway," Quigley said. "In fact, he knew quite a bit about my family, even though he hadn't seen my parents in years. And . . ."

"And?" Violet said.

Quigley gave her a small smile. "And he was very well-read," he said. "In fact, he was at Dr. Montgomery's house to do a bit more reading. He said there was an important file that was hidden someplace on the premises, and he had to stay for a few days to try and complete his investigation."

"So he didn't take you to the school?" Violet asked.

"He said it wasn't safe for me to be seen," Quigley said. "He explained that he was part of a secret organization, and that my parents had been a part of it, too."

"V.F.D.," Klaus said, and Quigley nodded in agreement.

"Duncan and Isadora tried to tell us about V.F.D.," Violet said, "but they never got the chance. We don't even know what it stands for."

"It seems to stand for many things," Quigley said, flipping pages in his notebook. "Nearly everything the organization uses, from the Volunteer Feline Detectives to the Vernacularly Fastened Door, has the same initials."

"But what is the organization?" Violet asked. "What is V.F.D.?"

"Jacques wouldn't tell me," Quigley said, "but I think the letters stand for Volunteer Fire Department."

"Volunteer Fire Department," Violet repeated, and looked at her brother. "What does that mean?"

"In some communities," Klaus said, "there's no official fire department, and so they rely on volunteers to extinguish fires."

"I know that," Violet said, "but what does that have to do with our parents, or Count Olaf, or anything that has happened to us? I always thought that knowing what the letters stood for would solve the mystery, but I'm as mystified as I ever was."

"Do you think our parents were secretly fighting fires?" Klaus asked.

"But why would they keep it a secret?" Violet asked. "And why would they have a secret passageway underneath the house?"

"Jacques said that the passageways were built by members of the organization," Quigley said. "In the case of an emergency, they could escape to a safe place."

"But the tunnel we found connects our house to the home of Esmé Squalor," Klaus said. "That's not a safe place."

"Something happened," Quigley said. "Something that changed everything." He flipped through a few pages of his commonplace book until he found what he was looking for. "Jacques Snicket called it a 'schism,'" he said, "but I don't know what that word means."

"A schism," Klaus said, "is a division of a

previously united group of people into two or more oppositional parties. It's like a big argument, with everybody choosing sides."

"That makes sense," Quigley said. "The way Jacques talked, it sounded like the entire organization was in chaos. Volunteers who were once working together are now enemies. Places that were once safe are now dangerous. Both sides are using the same codes, and the same disguises. Even the V.F.D. insignia used to represent the noble ideals everyone shared, but now it's all gone up in smoke."

"But how did the schism start?" Violet asked. "What was everyone fighting over?"

"I don't know," Quigley said. "Jacques didn't have much time to explain things to me."

"What was he doing?" Klaus asked.

"He was looking for you," Quigley replied. "He showed me a picture of all three of you, waiting at the dock on some lake, and asked me if I'd seen you anywhere. He knew that you'd been placed in Count Olaf's care, and all the terrible things that had happened there. He knew that you had gone to live with Dr. Montgomery. He even knew about some of the inventions you made, Violet, and the research you did, Klaus, and some of Sunny's tooth-related exploits. He wanted to find you before it was too late."

"Too late for what?" Violet said.

"I don't know," Quigley said with a sigh. "Jacques spent a long time at Dr. Montgomery's house, but he was too busy conducting his investigation to explain everything to me. He would stay up all night reading and copying information into his notebook, and then sleep all day, or disappear for hours at a time. And then one day, he said he had to go interview someone in the town of Paltryville, but he never came back. I waited weeks and weeks for him to return. I read books in Dr. Montgomery's library, and started a commonplace book of my own. At first it was difficult to find any information on V.F.D., but I took notes on anything I could find. I must have read hundreds of books, but Jacques never returned. Finally, one morning, two things happened that made me decide not to wait any longer. The first was an article in *The Daily Punctilio* saying that my siblings had been kidnapped from the school. I knew I had to do something. I couldn't wait for Jacques Snicket or for anyone else."

The Baudelaires nodded in solemn agreement. "What was the second thing?" Violet asked.

Quigley was silent for a moment, and he reached down to the ground and scooped up a handful of ashes, letting them fall from his gloved hands. "I smelled smoke," he said, "and when I opened the door of the Reptile Room, I saw that someone had thrown a torch through the glass of the ceiling, starting a fire in the library. Within minutes, the entire house was in flames."

"Oh," Violet said quietly. "Oh" is a word which usually means something along the lines

of, "I heard you, and I'm not particularly interested," but in this case, of course, the eldest
Baudelaire meant something entirely different,
and it is something that is difficult to define. She
meant "I am sad to hear that Uncle Monty's
house burned down," but that is not all. By "Oh,"
Violet was also trying to describe her sadness
about all of the fires that had brought Quigley
and Klaus and herself here to the Mortmain
Mountains, to huddle in a circle and try to solve
the mystery that surrounded them. When Violet
said "Oh," she was not only thinking of the fire
in the Reptile Room, but the fires that had
destroyed the Baudelaire home, and the Quagmire home, and Heimlich Hospital, and Caligari
Carnival, and the V.F.D. headquarters, where the
smell of smoke still lingered around where the
children were sitting. Thinking of all those fires
made Violet feel as if the entire world were going
up in flames, and that she and her siblings and
all the other decent people in the world might

never find a place that was truly safe.

"Another fire," Klaus murmured, and Violet knew he was thinking the same thing. "Where could you go, Quigley?"

"The only place I could think of was Paltry-ville," Quigley said. "The last time I saw Jacques, he'd said he was going there. I thought if I went there I might find him again, and see if he could help me rescue Duncan and Isadora. Dr. Mont-gomery's atlas showed me how to get there, but I had to go on foot, because I was afraid that anyone who might offer me a ride would be an enemy. It was a long time before I finally arrived, but as soon as I stepped into town I saw a large building that matched the tattoo on Jacques Snicket's ankle. I thought it might be a safe place to go."

"Dr. Orwell's office!" Klaus cried. "That's not a safe place to go!"

"Klaus was hypnotized there," Violet ex-plained, "and Count Olaf was disguised as—"

"As a receptionist," Quigley finished. "I know. His fake nameplate was still on the desk. The office was deserted, but I could tell that Jacques had been there, because there were some notes in his handwriting that he'd left on the desk. With those notes, and the information I'd read in Dr. Montgomery's library, I learned about the V.F.D. headquarters. So instead of waiting for Jacques again, I set out to find the organization. I thought they were my best hope of rescuing my siblings."

"So you set off to the Mortmain Mountains by yourself?" Violet asked.

"Not quite by myself," Quigley said. "I had this backpack that Jacques left behind, with the Verdant Flammable Devices and a few other items, and I had my commonplace book. And eventually, I ran into the Snow Scouts, and realized that hiding among them would be the quickest way to reach Mount Fraught." He turned a page in his commonplace book and examined his notes. "*Remarkable Phenomena of the Mortmain Mountains*, which I read in Dr. Montgomery's library, had a hidden chapter that told me all about the Vertical Flame Diversion and the Vernacularly Fastened Door."

Klaus looked over Quigley's shoulder to read his notes. "I should have read that book when I had the chance," he said, shaking his head. "If we had known about V.F.D. when we were living with Uncle Monty, we might have avoided all the trouble that followed."

"When we were living with Uncle Monty," Violet reminded him, "we were too busy trying to escape Count Olaf's clutches to do any additional research."

"I've had plenty of time to do research," Quigley said, "but I still haven't found all the answers I'm looking for. I still haven't found Duncan and Isadora, and I still don't know where Jacques Snicket is."

"He's dead," Klaus said, very quietly. "Count Olaf murdered him."

"I thought you might say that," Quigley said. "I knew something was very wrong when he didn't return. But what about my siblings? Do you know what happened to them?"

"They're safe, Quigley," Violet said. "We think they're safe. We rescued them from Olaf's clutches, and they escaped with a man named Hector."

"Escaped?" Quigley repeated. "Where did they go?"

"We don't know," Klaus admitted. "Hector built a self-sustaining hot air mobile home. It was like a flying house, kept in the air by a bunch of balloons, and Hector said it could stay up in the sky forever."

"We tried to climb aboard," Violet said, "but Count Olaf managed to stop us."

"So you don't know where they are?" Quigley asked.

"I'm afraid not," Violet said, and patted his hand. "But Duncan and Isadora are intrepid people, Quigley. They survived for quite some time in Olaf's clutches, taking notes on his schemes and trying to pass on the information to us."

"Violet's right," Klaus said. "I'm sure that wherever they are, they're continuing their research. Eventually, they'll find out you're alive, and they'll come looking for you, just like you went looking for them."

The two Baudelaires looked at one another and shivered. They had been talking about Quigley's family, of course, but they felt as if they were talking about their own. "I'm sure that if your parents are alive, they're looking for you, too," Quigley said, as if he'd read their minds. "And Sunny, too. Do you know where she is?"

"Someplace nearby," Violet said. "She's with Count Olaf, and Olaf wanted to find the headquarters, too."

"Maybe Olaf has already been here," Quigley said, looking around at the wreckage. "Maybe he's the one who burned this place down."

"I don't think so," Klaus said. "He wouldn't have had time to burn this whole place down. We were right on his trail. Plus, I don't think this place burned down all at once."

"Why not?" Quigley said.

"It's too big," Klaus replied. "If the whole headquarters were burning, the sky would be covered in smoke."

"That's true," Violet said. "That much smoke would arouse too much suspicion."

"Where there's smoke," Quigley said, "there's fire."

Violet and Klaus turned to their friend to agree, but Quigley was not looking at the two Baudelaires. He was looking past them, toward the frozen pool and the two frozen tributaries, where the enormous windows of the V.F.D. kitchen had once stood, and where I once chopped broccoli while the woman I loved mixed up a spicy peanut sauce to go with it, and he was pointing up toward the sky, where my associates and I used to watch the volunteer eagles who could spot smoke from a very great distance.

That afternoon, there were no eagles in the skies over the Mortmain Mountains, but as Violet and Klaus stood up and looked in the direction Quigley was pointing, there was something in the sky that caught their attention. Because when Quigley Quagmire said, "Where there's smoke, there's fire," he was not referring to Klaus's theory about the destruction of V.F.D. headquarters. He was talking about the sight of green smoke, wafting up into the sky from the peak of Mount Fraught, at the top of the slippery slope.

CHAPTER Nine

The two elder Baudelaires stood
for a moment with Quigley, gazing up at the small plume, a word
which here means "mysterious
cloud of green smoke." After the
long, strange story he had told
them about surviving the fire and
what he had learned about V.F.D.,
they could scarcely believe that
they were confronting another
mystery.

"It's a Verdant Flammable
Device," Quigley said. "There's
someone at the top of the waterfall, sending a signal."

"Yes," Violet said, "but who?"

"Maybe it's a volunteer, who escaped from the fire," Klaus said. "They're signaling to see if there are any other volunteers nearby."

"Or it could be a trap," Quigley said. "They could be luring volunteers up to the peak in order to ambush them. Remember, the codes of V.F.D. are used by both sides of the schism."

"It hardly seems like a code," Violet said. "We know that someone is communicating, but we don't have the faintest idea who they are, or what they're saying."

"This is what it must be like," Klaus said thoughtfully, "when Sunny talks to people who don't know her very well."

At the mention of Sunny's name, the Baudelaires were reminded of how much they missed her. "Whether it's a volunteer or a trap," Violet said, "it might be our only chance to find our sister."

"Or my sister and brother," Quigley said.

"Let's signal back," Klaus said. "Do you

still have those Verdant Flammable Devices, Quigley?"

"Of course," Quigley said, taking the box of green tubes out of his backpack, "but Bruce saw my matches and confiscated them, because children shouldn't play with matches."

"Confiscated them?" Klaus said. "Do you think he's an enemy of V.F.D.?"

"If everyone who said that children shouldn't play with matches was an enemy of V.F.D.," Violet said with a smile, "then we wouldn't have a chance of survival."

"But how are we going to light these without matches?" Quigley asked.

Violet reached into her pocket. It was a bit tricky to tie her hair up in a ribbon, as all four drafts in the Valley of Four Drafts were blowing hard, but at last her hair was out of her eyes, and the gears and levers of her inventing mind began to move as she gazed up at the mysterious signal.

But of course this signal was neither a volunteer nor a trap. It was a baby, with unusually large teeth and a way of talking that some people found confusing. When Sunny Baudelaire had said "lox," for example, the members of Count Olaf's troupe had assumed she was simply babbling, rather than explaining how she was going to cook the salmon that the hook-handed man had caught. "Lox" is a word which refers to smoked salmon, and it is a delicious way to enjoy freshly caught fish, particularly if one has the appropriate accoutrements, a phrase which here means "bagels, cream cheese, sliced cucumber, black pepper, and capers, which can be eaten along with the lox for an enjoyable meal." Lox also has an additional benefit of producing quite a bit of smoke as it is prepared, and this is the reason Sunny chose this method of preparing salmon, as opposed to gravlax, which is salmon marinated for several days in a mixture of spices, or sashimi, which is salmon cut into pleasing shapes and simply served raw. Remembering what Count Olaf had said about being able to see everything and everyone from the peak where he had brought her, the youngest Baudelaire realized that the phrase "where there's smoke there's fire" might be able to help her. As Violet and Klaus heard Quigley's extraordinary tale at the bottom of the frozen waterfall, Sunny hurried to prepare lox and send a signal to her siblings, who she hoped were nearby. First, she nudged the Verdant Flammable Device—which she, like everyone at the peak, believed was a cigarette—into a small patch of weeds, in order to increase the smoke. Then she dragged over the covered casserole dish that she had been using as a makeshift bed, and placed the salmon inside it. In no time at all, the fish caught by the hook-handed man were absorbing the heat and smoke from the simmering green tube, and a large plume of green smoke was floating up into the sky above Mount Fraught. Sunny gazed up at the signal she made and couldn't help smiling. The last time she had been separated from her siblings, she had simply waited in the birdcage for them to come and rescue her, but she had grown since then, and was able to take an active part in defeating Count Olaf and his troupe, while still having time to prepare a seafood dish.

"Something smells delicious," said one of the white-faced women, walking by the casserole dish. "I must admit, I had some doubts that an infant should be in charge of the cooking, but your salmon recipe seems like it will be very tasty indeed."

"There's a word for the way she's preparing the fish," the hook-handed man said, "but I can't remember what it is."

"*Lox*," Sunny said, but no one heard her over the sound of Count Olaf storming out of his tent, followed by Esmé and the two sinister visitors. Olaf was clutching the Snicket file and glaring down at Sunny with his shiny, shiny eyes.

"Put that smoke out *at once*!" he ordered. "I thought you were a terrified orphan prisoner, but I'm beginning to think you're a spy!"

"What do you mean, Olaf?" asked the other white-faced woman. "She's using Esmé's cigarette to cook us some fish."

"Someone might see the smoke," Esmé snarled, as if she had not been smoking herself just moments ago. "Where there's smoke, there's fire."

The man with a beard but no hair picked up a handful of snow and threw it onto the weeds, extinguishing the Verdant Flammable Device. "Who are you signaling to, baby?" he asked, in his strange, hoarse voice. "If you're a spy, we're going to toss you off this mountain."

"Goo goo," Sunny said, which meant something along the lines of "I'm going to pretend I'm a helpless baby, instead of answering your question."

"You see?" the white-faced woman said, looking nervously at the man with a beard but no hair. "She's just a helpless baby."

"Perhaps you're right," said the woman with

hair but no beard. "Besides, there's no reason to toss a baby off a mountain unless you absolutely have to."

"Babies can come in handy," Count Olaf agreed. "In fact, I've been thinking about recruiting more young people into my troupe. They're less likely to complain about doing my bidding."

"But we never complain," the hook-handed man said. "I try to be as accommodating as possible."

"Enough chitchat," said the man with a beard but no hair. "We have a lot of scheming to do, Olaf. I have some information that might help you with your recruiting idea, and according to the Snicket file, there's one more safe place for the volunteers to gather."

"The last safe place," said the sinister woman. "We have to find it and burn it down."

"And once we do," Count Olaf said, "the last evidence of our plans will be completely destroyed. We'll never have to worry about the authorities again."

"Where is this last safe place?" asked Kevin.

Olaf opened his mouth to answer, but the woman with hair but no beard stopped him with a quick gesture and a suspicious glance down at Sunny. "Not in front of the toothy orphan," she said, in her deep, deep voice. "If she learned what we were up to, she'd never sleep again, and you need your infant servant full of energy. Send her away, and we'll make our plans."

"Of course," Olaf said, smiling nervously at the sinister visitors. "Orphan, go to my car and remove all of the potato chip crumbs from the interior by blowing as hard as you can."

"Futil," Sunny said, which meant something like, "That is an absolutely impossible chore," but she walked unsteadily toward the car while Olaf's troupe laughed and gathered around the flat rock to hear the new scheme. Passing the extinguished fire and the covered casserole dish where she would sleep that night, Sunny sighed sadly, thinking that her signal plan must have failed. But when she reached Olaf's car and gazed down at the frozen waterfall, she saw something that lightened her spirits, a phrase which here means "an identical plume of green smoke, coming from the very bottom of the slope." The youngest Baudelaire looked down at the smoke and smiled. "Sibling," she said to herself. Sunny, of course, could not be certain that it was Violet and Klaus who were signaling to her, but she could hope it was so, and hope was enough to cheer her up as she opened the door of the car and began blowing at the crumbs Olaf and his troupe had scattered all over the upholstery.

But at the bottom of the frozen waterfall, the two elder Baudelaires did not feel nearly as hopeful as they stood with Quigley and watched the green smoke disappear from the highest peak.

"Someone put out the Verdant Flammable Device," Quigley said, holding the green tube to one side so he wouldn't smell the smoke. "What do you think that means?"

"I don't know," Violet said, and sighed. "This isn't working."

"Of course it's working," Klaus said. "It's working perfectly. You noticed that the afternoon sun was reflecting off the frozen waterfall, and it gave you the idea to use the scientific principles of the convergence and refraction of light—just like you did on Lake Lachrymose, when we were battling the leeches. So you used Colette's hand mirror to catch the sun's rays and reflect them onto the end of the Verdant Flammable Device, so we could light it and send a signal."

"Klaus is right," Quigley said. "It couldn't have worked better."

"Thank you," Violet said, "but that's not what I mean. I mean this code isn't working. We still don't know who's up on the peak, or why they were signaling us, and now the signal has stopped, but we still don't know what it means."

"Maybe we should extinguish our Verdant

Flammable Device, too," Klaus said.

"Maybe," Violet agreed, "or maybe we should go up to the top of the waterfall and see for ourselves who is there."

Quigley frowned, and took out his commonplace book. "The only way up to the highest peak," he said, "is the path that the Snow Scouts are taking. We'd have to go back through the Vernacularly Fastened Door, back down the Vertical Flame Diversion, back into the Volunteer Feline Detective cave, rejoin the scouts and hike for a long time."

"That's not the only way up to the peak," Violet said with a smile.

"Yes, it is," Quigley insisted. "Look at the map."

"Look at the waterfall," Violet replied, and all three children looked up at the shiny slope.

"Do you mean," Klaus said, "that you think you can invent something which can get us up a frozen waterfall?"

But Violet was already tying her hair out of

her eyes again, and looking around at the ruins of the V.F.D. headquarters. "I'll need that ukulele that you took from the caravan," she said to Klaus, "and that half-melted candelabra over there by the dining room table."

Klaus took the ukulele from his coat pocket and handed it to his sister, and then walked over to the table to retrieve the strange, melted object. "Unless you need any further assistance," he said, "I think I might go examine the wreckage of the library and see if any documents have survived. We might as well learn as much from this headquarters as we can."

"Good idea," Quigley said, and reached into his backpack. He brought out a notebook much like his own, except it had a dark blue cover. "I have a spare notebook," he said. "You might be interested in starting a commonplace book of your own."

"That's very kind of you," Klaus said. "I'll write down anything I find. Do you want to join the search?"

"I think I'll stay here," Quigley said, looking at Violet. "I've heard quite a bit about Violet Baudelaire's marvelous inventions, and I'd like to see her at work."

Klaus nodded, and walked off to the iron archway marking the entrance of the ruined library, while Violet blushed and leaned down to pick up one of the forks that had survived the fire.

It is one of the great sadnesses of the Baudelaire case that Violet never got to meet a man named C. M. Kornbluth, an associate of mine who spent most of his life living and working in the Valley of Four Drafts as a mechanical instructor at the V.F.D. headquarters. Mr. Kornbluth was a quiet and secretive man, so secretive that no one ever knew who he was, where he came from, or even what the C or the M stood for, and he spent much of his time holed up in his dormitory room writing strange stories, or gazing sadly out the windows of the kitchen. The one thing that put Mr. Kornbluth in a good mood would be a particularly promising mechanical student. If a young man showed an interest in deep sea radar, Mr. Kornbluth would take off his glasses and smile. If a young woman brought him a staple gun she had built, Mr. Kornbluth would clap his hands in excitement. And if a pair of twins asked him how to properly reroute some copper wiring, he would take a paper bag out of his pocket and offer some pistachio nuts to anyone who happened to be around. So, when I think of Violet Baudelaire standing in the wreckage of the V.F.D. headquarters, carefully taking the strings off the ukulele and bending some of the forks in half, I can imagine Mr. Kornbluth, even though he and his pistachios are long gone, turning from the window, smiling at the Baudelaire inventor, and saying, "Beatrice, come over here! Look at what this girl is making!"

"What are you making?" Quigley asked.

"Something that will get us up that waterfall," Violet replied. "I only wish that Sunny were here. Her teeth would be perfect to slice these ukulele strings into halves."

"I might have something that could help," Quigley said, looking through his backpack. "When I was in Dr. Orwell's office, I found these fake fingernails. They're a horrible shade of pink, but they're quite sharp."

Violet took a fingernail from Quigley and looked at it carefully. "I think Count Olaf was wearing these," she said, "as part of his receptionist disguise. It's so strange that you have been following in our footsteps all this time, and yet we never even knew you were alive."

"I knew you were alive," Quigley said. "Jacques Snicket told me all about you, Klaus, Sunny, and even your parents. He knew them quite well before you were born."

"I thought so," Violet said, cutting the ukulele strings. "In the photograph we found, my parents are standing with Jacques Snicket and another man."

"He's probably Jacques's brother," Quigley

said. "Jacques told me that he was working closely with his two siblings on an important file."

"The Snicket file," Violet said. "We were hoping to find it here."

Quigley looked up at the frozen waterfall. "Maybe whoever signaled us will know where it is," he said.

"We'll find out soon enough," Violet said. "Please take off your shoes."

"My shoes?" Quigley asked.

"The waterfall will be very slippery," Violet explained, "so I'm using the ukulele strings to tie these bent forks to the toe area, to make fork-assisted climbing shoes. We'll hold two more forks in our hands. Tines of the forks are almost as sharp as Sunny's teeth, so the fork-assisted climbing shoes will easily dig into the ice with each step, and enable us to keep our balance."

"But what's the candelabra for?" Quigley asked, unlacing his shoes.

"I'm going to use it as an ice tester," Violet

said. "A moving body of water, such as a water-fall, is rarely completely frozen. There are probably places on that slope where there is only a thin layer of ice, particularly with False Spring on its way. If we stuck our forks through the ice and hit water, we'd lose our grip and fall. So I'll tap on the ice with the candelabra before each step, to find the solid places we should climb."

"It sounds like a difficult journey," Quigley said.

"No more difficult than climbing up the Vertical Flame Diversion," Violet said, tying a fork onto Quigley's shoe. "I'm using the Sumac knot, so it should hold tight. Now, all we need is Klaus's shoes, and—"

"I'm sorry to interrupt, but I think this might be important," Klaus said, and Violet turned to see that her brother had returned. He was holding the dark blue notebook in one hand and a small, burnt piece of paper in the other. "I found this scrap of paper in a pile of ashes," he said. "It's from some kind of code book."

"What does it say?" Violet asked.

"'In the e   flagration resulting in the destruction of a sanc   ,'" Klaus read, "'   teers should avail themselves of Verbal Fri   Dialogue, which is concealed accordingly.'"

"That doesn't make any sense," Quigley said. "Do you think it's in code?"

"Sort of," Klaus said. "Parts of the sentence are burned away, so you have to figure the sentence out as if it's encoded. 'Flagration' is probably the last part of the word 'conflagration,' a fancy word for fire, and 'sanc' is probably the beginning of the word 'sanctuary,' which means a safe place. So the sentence probably began something like, 'In the event of a conflagration resulting in the destruction of a sanctuary.'"

Violet stood up and looked over his shoulder. "'Teers,'" she said, "is probably 'volunteers,' but I don't know what 'avail themselves' means."

"It means 'to make use of,'" Klaus said, "like you're availing yourself of the ukulele and those forks. Don't you see? This says that in case a safe place burns down, they'll leave some sort of message—'Verbal Fri   Dialogue.'"

"But what could 'Verbal Fri   Dialogue' be?" Quigley asked. "Friends? Frisky?"

"Frilly?" Violet guessed. "Frightening?"

"But it says that it's concealed accordingly," Klaus pointed out. "That means that the dialogue is hidden in a logical way. If it were Verbal Waterfall Dialogue, it would be hidden in the waterfall. So none of those words can be right. Where would someone leave a message where fire couldn't destroy it?"

"But fire destroys everything," Violet said. "Look at the headquarters. Nothing is left standing except the library entrance, and . . ."

". . . and the refrigerator," Klaus finished. "Or, we might say, the fridge."

"Verbal Fridge Dialogue!" Quigley said.

"The volunteers left a message," said Klaus, who was already halfway to the refrigerator, "in the only place they knew wouldn't be affected by the fire."

"And the one place their enemies wouldn't think of looking," Quigley said. "After all, there's never anything terribly important in the refrigerator."

What Quigley said, of course, is not entirely true. Like an envelope, a hollow figurine, and a coffin, a refrigerator can hold all sorts of things, and they may turn out to be very important depending on what kind of day you are having. A refrigerator may hold an icepack, for example, which would be important if you had been wounded. A refrigerator may hold a bottle of water, which would be important if you were dying of thirst. And a refrigerator may hold a basket of strawberries, which would be important if a maniac said to you, "If you don't give me a basket of strawberries right now, I'm going to poke you with this large stick." But when the two elder Baudelaires and Quigley Quagmire opened the refrigerator, they found nothing that would help someone who was wounded, dying of thirst, or being threatened by a strawberry-crazed, stick-carrying maniac, or anything that looked important at all. The fridge was mostly empty, with just a few of the usual things people keep in their refrigerators and rarely use, including a jar of mustard, a container of olives, three jars of different kinds of jam, a bottle of lemon juice, and one lonely pickle in a small glass jug.

"There's nothing here," Violet said.

"Look in the crisper," Quigley said, pointing to a drawer in the refrigerator traditionally used for storing fruits and vegetables. Klaus opened the drawer and pulled out a few strands of a green plant with tiny, skinny leaves.

"It smells like dill," Klaus said, "and it's quite crisp, as if it were picked yesterday."

"Very Fresh Dill," Quigley said.

"Another mystery," Violet said, and tears filled her eyes. "We have nothing but mysteries. We don't know where Sunny is. We don't know where Count Olaf is. We don't know who's signaling to us at the top of the waterfall, or what they're trying to say, and now there's a mysterious message in a mysterious code in a mysterious refrigerator, and a bunch of mysterious herbs in the crisper. I'm tired of mysteries. I want someone to help us."

"We can help each other," Klaus said. "We have your inventions, and Quigley's maps, and my research."

"And we're all very well-read," Quigley said. "That should be enough to solve any mystery."

Violet sighed, and kicked at something that lay on the ashen ground. It was the small shell of a pistachio nut, blackened from the fire that destroyed the headquarters. "It's like we're members of V.F.D. already," she said. "We're sending signals, and breaking codes, and finding secrets in the ruins of a fire."

"Do you think our parents would be proud of us," Klaus asked, "for following in their footsteps?"

"I don't know," Violet said. "After all, they kept V.F.D. a secret."

"Maybe they were going to tell us later," Klaus said.

"Or maybe they hoped we would never find out," Violet said.

"I keep wondering the same thing," Quigley said. "If I could travel back in time to the moment my mother showed me the secret passageway under the library, I would ask her why she was keeping these secrets."

"That's one more mystery," Violet said sadly, and looked up at the slippery slope. It was getting later and later in the afternoon, and the frozen waterfall looked less and less shiny in the fading sunlight, as if time were running out to climb to the top and see who had been signaling to them. "We should each investigate the mystery we're most likely to solve," she said. "I'll climb up the waterfall, and solve the mystery of the Verdant Flammable Device by learning who's up there, and what they want. You should stay down here, Klaus, and solve the mystery of the Verbal Fridge Dialogue, by learning the code and discovering what the message is."

"And I'll help you both," Quigley said, taking out his purple notebook. "I'll leave my commonplace book with Klaus, in case it's any help with the codes. And I'll climb up the waterfall with you, Violet, in case you need my help."

"Are you sure?" Violet asked. "You've already taken us this far, Quigley. You don't have to risk your life any further."

"We'll understand," Klaus said, "if you want to leave and search for your siblings."

"Don't be absurd," Quigley said. "We're all part of this mystery, whatever it is. Of course I'm going to help you."

The two Baudelaires looked at one another and smiled. It is so rare in this world to meet a trustworthy person who truly wants to help you, and finding such a person can make you feel warm and safe, even if you are in the middle of a windy valley high up in the mountains. For a moment, as their friend smiled back at them, it seemed as if all the mysteries had been solved already, even with Sunny still separated from them, and Count Olaf still at large, and the abandoned V.F.D. headquarters still in ashes around them. Just knowing that they had found a person like Quigley Quagmire made Violet and Klaus feel as if every code made sense, and every signal was clear.

Violet stepped forward, her fork-assisted climbing shoes making small, determined noises on the ground, and took Quigley's hand. "Thank you," she said, "for volunteering."

CHAPTER
Ten

Violet and Quigley walked carefully across the frozen pool until they reached the bottom of the waterfall. "Good luck!" Klaus called, from the archway of the ruined library. He was polishing his glasses, as he often did before embarking on serious research.

"Good luck to you!" Violet replied, shouting over the rush of the mountain winds, and as she looked back at her brother, she remembered when the two siblings were trying to stop the caravan as it hurtled down the mountain. Klaus had wanted to say something to her, in case the drag chute and the mixture of sticky substances hadn't worked. Violet had the same feeling now, as she prepared to climb the frozen waterfall and leave her brother behind at the ashy remains of the V.F.D. headquarters. "Klaus—" she said.

Klaus put his glasses on and gave his sister his bravest smile. "Whatever you're thinking of saying," he said, "say it when you return."

Violet nodded, and tapped the candelabra against a spot on the ice. She heard a deep *thunk!,* as if she were tapping something very solid. "We'll start here," she said to Quigley. "Brace yourself."

The expression "brace yourself," as I'm sure you know, does not mean to take some metal

wiring and rivets and other orthodontic materials and apply them to your own teeth in order
to straighten them. The expression simply
means "get ready for something that will probably be difficult,"and it was indeed very difficult to climb a frozen waterfall in the middle of
a windswept valley with nothing but a candelabra and a few well-placed forks to aid the two
children in their climb. It took a few moments
for Violet and Quigley to work her invention
properly, and push the forks into the ice just far
enough to hold them there, but not so far that
they would be permanently stuck, and once
both of them were in position, Violet had to
reach up as far as she could and tap the candelabra on the ice above them to find the next
solid place to climb. For the first few steps, it
seemed like ascending the icy slope in this manner would be impossible, but as time went on,
and the two volunteers grew more and more
skillful with the fork-tipped climbing shoes and

the candelabra ice-tester, it became clear that once again Violet's inventing skills would carry the day, a phrase which here means "enable Violet Baudelaire and Quigley Quagmire to climb up a frozen waterfall after bracing themselves for the difficult journey."

"Your invention is working," Quigley called up to Violet. "These fork-assisted climbing shoes are marvelous."

"They do seem to be working," Violet agreed, "but let's not celebrate just yet. We have a long way to go."

"My sister wrote a couplet about that very thing," Quigley said, and recited Isadora's poem:

"Celebrate when you're half-done,
And the finish won't be half as fun."

Violet smiled, and reached up to test the ice above her. "Isadora is a good poet," Violet said, "and her poems have come in handy more than once. When we were at the Village of Fowl

Devotees, she led us to her location by hiding a secret message in a series of couplets."

"I wonder if that's a code she learned from V.F.D.," Quigley said, "or if she made it up herself."

"I don't know," Violet said thoughtfully. "She and Duncan were the first to tell us about V.F.D., but it never occurred to me that they might already be members. When I think about it, however, the code she used was similar to one that our Aunt Josephine used. They both hid a secret location within a note, and waited for us to discover the hidden message. Maybe they were all volunteers." She removed her left fork-assisted climbing shoe from the ice, and kicked it back in a few inches up to further her climb. "Maybe all our guardians have been members of V.F.D., on one side or the other of the schism."

"It's hard to believe," Quigley said, "that we've always been surrounded by people carrying out secret errands, and never known it."

"It's hard to believe that we're climbing a

frozen waterfall in the Mortmain Mountains," Violet replied, "and yet, here we are. There, Quigley, do you see the ledge where my left fork is? It's solid enough for both of us to sit for a moment and catch our breath."

"Good," Quigley said. "I have a small bag of carrots in my backpack we can eat to regain our energy." The triplet climbed up to where Violet was sitting, on a small ledge scarcely the size of a sofa, and slid so he was sitting next to her. The two climbers could see that they had traveled farther than they'd thought. Far below them were the blackened ruins of the headquarters, and Klaus was only a small speck near a tiny iron archway. Quigley handed Violet a carrot, and she bit down on it thoughtfully.

"Sunny loves raw carrots," Violet said. "I hope that she's eating well, wherever she is."

"I hope my siblings are eating well, too," Quigley said. "My father always used to say that a good meal can cheer one up considerably."

"My father always said the same thing," Violet said, looking at Quigley curiously. "Do you think *that* was a code, too?"

Quigley shrugged and sighed. Small bits of ice from the waterfall fell from the ends of forks and blew away in the wind. "It's like we never really knew our parents," he said.

"We knew them," Violet said. "They just had a few secrets, that's all. Everyone should keep a few secrets."

"I suppose so," Quigley said, "but they might have mentioned that they were in a secret organization with a headquarters hidden in the Mortmain Mountains."

"Maybe they didn't want us to find out about such a dangerous place," Violet said, peering off the ledge, "although if you have to hide a headquarters, it's a beautiful place to do it. Aside from the remains of the fire, this is a very lovely view."

"Very lovely indeed," Quigley said, but he

was not looking at the view beneath him. He was looking beside him, where Violet Baudelaire was sitting.

Many things have been taken from the three Baudelaires. Their parents were taken, of course, and their home was taken from them, by a terrible fire. Their various guardians were taken from them, because they were murdered by Count Olaf or were simply miserable guardians who soon lost interest in three young children with nowhere to go. The Baudelaires' dignity was taken from them, on the occasions when the siblings were forced to wear absurd disguises, and recently they had been taken from one another, with the kidnapped Sunny doing chores at the top of the frozen waterfall while Violet and Klaus learned the secrets of V.F.D. at the bottom. But one thing that was taken from the Baudelaires that is not often discussed is their privacy, a word which here means "time by oneself, without anyone watching or interfering." Unless you are a hermit or half of a pair of

Siamese twins, you probably enjoy taking the occasional break from members of your family to enjoy some privacy, perhaps with a friend or companion, in your room or in a railway car you have managed to sneak aboard. But since that dreadful day at Briny Beach, when Mr. Poe arrived to tell the Baudelaires that their parents had perished, the three children had scarcely had any privacy at all. From the small, dark bedroom where they slept at Count Olaf's house, to the crowded caravan at Caligari Carnival, and all of the other woeful places in between, the Baudelaires' situation was always so desperate and cramped that they were rarely able to spare a moment for a bit of private time.

So, as Violet and Quigley rest for a few minutes more on a ledge halfway up the frozen waterfall, I will take this opportunity to give them a bit of privacy, by not writing down anything more of what happened between these two friends on that chilly afternoon. Certainly there are aspects of my own personal life that I

will never write down, however precious they are to me, and I will offer the eldest Baudelaire the same courtesy. I will tell you that the two young people resumed their climb, and that the afternoon slowly turned to evening and that both Violet and Quigley had small secret smiles on their faces as the candelabra ice-tester and the fork-assisted climbing shoes helped them both get closer and closer to the mountains' highest peak, but there has been so little privacy in the life of Violet Baudelaire that I will allow her to keep a few important moments to herself, rather than sharing them with my distressed and weeping readers.

"We're almost there," Violet said. "It's difficult to see with the sun going down, but I believe we're just about at the top of the peak."

"I can't believe we've been climbing all afternoon," Quigley said.

"Not *all* afternoon," she reminded him with a shy smile. "I guess this waterfall is about as high as 667 Dark Avenue. It took a very long time to go up and down that elevator shaft, trying to rescue your siblings. I hope this is a more successful journey."

"Me, too," Quigley said. "What do you think we will find at the top?"

"Set!" came the reply.

"I couldn't hear you over the wind," Quigley said. "What did you say?"

"I didn't say anything," Violet said. She squinted above her, trying to see in the last of the sunset, and scarcely daring to hope that she had heard correctly.

Out of all the words in the English language, the word "set" has the most definitions, and if you open a good dictionary and read the word's long, long entry, you will begin to think that "set" is scarcely a word at all, only a sound that means something different depending on who is saying it. If a group of jazz musicians says "set," for instance, they are probably referring to the songs they are planning to play at a club that evening, assuming it doesn't burn down. If the owner of a restaurant uses the word "set," they might mean a group of matching wineglasses, or a bunch of waitresses who look exactly alike. A librarian will say "set" to refer to a collection of books that are all by the same author or about the same subject, and an Egyptologist will use the word "set" to refer to the ancient god of evil, although he does not come up very often in conversation. But when Violet heard the word "set" from the top of Mount Fraught, she did not think there was a group of jazz musicians, a restaurant owner, a librarian, or an Egyptologist talking about jazz tunes, wineglasses, waitresses, thematically linked books, or a black, immoral aardvark who is the sworn enemy of the god Osiris. She reached her fork as high as she could so she could climb closer, and saw the rays of the sunset reflect off a large tooth, and Violet knew that this time, the definition of "set" was "I knew you would find me!" and the speaker was Sunny Baudelaire.

"Set!" Sunny said again.

"Sunny!" Violet cried.

"Sssh!" Sunny said.

"What is going on?" Quigley asked, several forksteps behind Violet.

"It's Sunny," Violet said, and hoisted herself onto the peak to see her baby sister, standing next to Count Olaf's car and grinning from ear to ear. Without another word, the two Baudelaire sisters hugged fiercely, Violet taking care not to poke Sunny with one of the forks she was holding. By the time Quigley reached the top of the peak and pulled himself up to lean against one of the car's tires, the two Baudelaires were smiling at each other with tears in their eyes.

"I knew we'd see you again, Sunny," Violet said. "I just knew it."

"Klaus?" Sunny asked.

"He's safe and nearby," Violet said. "He knew we could find you, too."

"Set," Sunny agreed, but then she noticed Quigley and her eyes grew wide. "Quagmire?" she asked in amazement.

"Yes," Violet said. "This is Quigley Quagmire, Sunny. He survived the fire after all." Sunny walked unsteadily over to Quigley and shook his hand. "He led us to the headquarters, Sunny, with a map he drew himself."

"Arigato," Sunny said, which meant something like, "I appreciate your help, Quigley."

"Was it you who signaled us?" Quigley asked.

"Yep," Sunny said. "Lox."

"Count Olaf's been making you do the cooking?" Violet asked in amazement.

"Vaccurum," Sunny said.

"Olaf even made her clean crumbs out of the car," Violet translated to Quigley, "by blowing as hard as she could."

"That's ridiculous!" Quigley said.

"Cinderella," Sunny said. She meant something along the lines of, "I've had to do all of the chores, while being humiliated at every turn," but Violet had no time to translate over the sound of Count Olaf's scratchy voice.

"Where are you, Babylaire?" he asked, adding

an absurd nickname to his list of insults. "I've thought of more tasks for you to perform."

The three children looked at one another in panic. "Hide," Sunny whispered, and there was no need for translation. Violet and Quigley looked around the desolate landscape of the peak for a place to hide, but there was only one place to go.

"Under the car," Violet said, and she and Quigley wriggled underneath the long, black automobile, which was as dirty and smelly as its owner. As an inventor, the eldest Baudelaire had stared closely at automotive machinery plenty of times, but she had never seen such an extreme state of disrepair, a phrase which here means "an underside of an automobile in such bad shape that it was dripping oil on her and her companion." But Violet and Quigley didn't have a moment to waste thinking of their discomfort. They had no sooner moved their fork-assisted climbing shoes out of view when Count Olaf and his companions arrived. From underneath the car, the two volunteers could see only the villain's tattoo on the filthy ankle above his left shoe, and a pair of very stylish pumps, decorated with glitter and tiny paintings of eyes, that could only belong to Esmé Squalor.

"All we've had to eat all day is that smoked salmon, and it's almost dinnertime," Count Olaf said. "You'd better get cooking, orphan."

"Tomorrow is False Spring," Esmé said, "and it would be very in to have a False Spring dinner."

"Did you hear that, toothy?" Olaf asked. "My girlfriend wants a stylish dinner. Get to work."

"Olaf, we need you," said a very deep voice, and Violet and Quigley saw two pairs of sinister black shoes appear behind the villain and his girlfriend, whose shoes twitched nervously at the sight of them. All of a sudden, it seemed much colder underneath the car, and Violet had to push her legs against the tires, so they would not shiver against the mechanics of the underside and be heard.

"Yes, Olaf," agreed the hoarse voice of the man with a beard but no hair, although Violet and Quigley could not see him. "Our recruitment plan will happen first thing in the morning, so we need you to help spread the net out on the ground."

"Can't you ask one of our employees?" asked Esmé. "There's the hook-handed man, the two white-faced women, and the three freaks we picked up at the carnival. That's eight people, if you include yourselves, to spread out the net. Why should we do it?"

The four black shoes stepped toward Esme's stylish pumps and Olaf's tattoo. "You'll do it," said the woman with hair but no beard, "because I say so."

There was a long, ominous pause, and then Count Olaf gave a little high-pitched laugh. "That's a good point," he said. "Come on, Esmé. We've bossed around the baby, so there's nothing else to do around here anyway."

"That's true," Esmé agreed. "In fact, I was

thinking about taking up smoking again, because I'm bored. Do you have any more of those green cigarettes?"

"I'm afraid not," replied the man with a beard but no hair, leading the villains away from the car. "That's the only one I found."

"That's too bad," Esmé said. "I don't like the taste or the smell, and they're very bad for you, but cigarettes are very in and I'd like to smoke another one."

"Maybe there's another one in the ruins of headquarters," said the woman with hair but no beard. "It's hard to find everything in all those ashes. We searched for days and couldn't find the sugar bowl."

"Not in front of the baby," Olaf said quickly, and the four pairs of shoes walked away. Violet and Quigley stayed underneath the car until Sunny said "Coastkleer," which meant something like, "It's safe to come out now."

"Those were terrible people," Quigley said with a shudder, brushing oil and grime off his coat. "They made me feel cold all over."

"They certainly had an aura of menace," Violet agreed in a whisper. "The feet with the tattoo were Count Olaf, and those glittery shoes were Esmé Squalor, but who were the other two, Sunny?"

"Unno Narsonist," Sunny murmured. She meant something along the lines of "I don't know, but they burned down V.F.D. headquarters," and Violet was quick to explain this to Quigley.

"Klaus has found an important message that survived the fire," Violet said. "By the time we take you down the waterfall, I'm sure he'll have decoded the message. Come on."

"Nogo," Sunny said, which meant "I don't think I ought to accompany you."

"Why on earth not?" Violet asked.

"Unasanc," Sunny said.

"Sunny says that the villains have mentioned one more safe place for volunteers to gather," Violet explained to Quigley.

"Do you know where it is?" Quigley asked.

Sunny shook her head. "Olafile," she said.

"But if Count Olaf has the Snicket file," Violet said, "how are you going to find out where this safe place is?"

"Matahari," she said, which meant something like, "If I stay, I can spy on them and find out."

"Absolutely not," Violet said, after she had translated. "It's not safe for you to stay here, Sunny. It's bad enough that Olaf has made you do the cooking."

"Lox," Sunny pointed out.

"But what are you going to make for a False Spring dinner?" Violet asked.

Sunny gave her sister a smile, and walked over to the trunk of the car. Violet and Quigley heard her rummaging around among the remaining groceries, but stayed put so Olaf or any of his associates wouldn't spot them. When Sunny returned, she had a triumphant smile on her face, and the frozen hunk of spinach, the large bag of mushrooms, the can of water chestnuts, and the enormous eggplant in her arms. "False spring rolls!" she said, which meant something like, "An assortment of vegetables wrapped in spinach leaves, prepared in honor of False Spring."

"I'm surprised you can even carry that eggplant, let alone prepare it," Violet said. "It must weigh as much as you do."

"Suppertunity," Sunny said. She meant something like, "Serving the troupe dinner will be a perfect chance to listen to their conversation," and Violet reluctantly translated.

"It sounds dangerous," Quigley said.

"Of course it's dangerous," Violet said. "If she's caught spying, who knows what they'll do?"

"Ga ga goo goo," Sunny said, which meant "I won't be caught, because they think I'm only a helpless baby."

"I think your sister is right," Quigley said. "It wouldn't be safe to carry her down the waterfall, anyway. We need our hands and feet for the climb. Let Sunny investigate the mystery she's most likely to solve, while we work on an escape plan."

Violet shook her head. "I don't want to leave my sister behind," she said. "The Baudelaires should never be separated."

"Separate Klaus," Sunny pointed out.

"If there's another place where volunteers are gathering," Quigley said, "we need to know where it is. Sunny can find out for us, but only if she stays here."

"I'm not going to leave my baby sister on top of a mountain," Violet said.

Sunny dropped her vegetables on the ground and walked over to her sister and smiled. "I'm not a baby," Sunny said, and hugged her. It was the longest sentence the youngest Baudelaire had ever said, and as Violet looked down at her sister, she saw how true it was. Sunny was not really a baby, not anymore. She was a young girl with unusually sharp teeth, some impressive cooking skills, and an opportunity to spy on a group of villains and discover a piece of crucial information. Sometime, during the unfortunate events that had befallen the three orphans, Sunny had grown out of her babyhood, and although it made Violet a bit sad to think about it, it made her proud, too, and she gave her sister a smile.

"I guess you're right," Violet said. "You're not a baby. But be careful, Sunny. You're a young girl, but it's still quite dangerous for a young girl to spy on villains. And remember, we're right at the bottom of the slope, Sunny. If you need us, just signal again."

Sunny opened her mouth to reply, but before she could utter a sound, the three children heard a long, lazy hissing noise from underneath Olaf's car, as if one of Dr. Montgomery's snakes were hiding there. The car shifted lightly, and Violet pointed to one of Olaf's tires, which had gone flat. "I must have punctured it," Violet said, "with my fork-assisted climbing shoes."

"I suppose that's not a nice thing to do,"

Quigley said, "but I can't say I'm sorry."

"How's dinner coming along, toothface?" called Count Olaf's cruel voice over the sound of the wind.

"I guess we'd better leave before we're discovered," Violet said, giving her sister one more hug and a kiss on the top of her head. "We'll see you soon, Sunny."

"Good-bye, Sunny," Quigley said. "I'm so glad we finally met in person. And thank you very much for helping us find the last safe place."

Sunny Baudelaire looked up at Quigley, and then at her older sister, and gave them both a big, happy smile that showed all of her impressive teeth. After spending so much time in the company of villains, she was happy to be with some people who respected her skills, appreciated her work, and understood her way of speaking. Even with Klaus still at the bottom of the waterfall, Sunny felt as if she had already been happily reunited with her family, and that her time in the Mortmain Mountains would have a happy ending. She was wrong about that, of course, but for now the youngest Baudelaire smiled up at these two people who cared about her, one she had just met and one she had known her entire life, and felt as if she were growing taller at that very moment.

"Happy," said the young girl, and everyone who heard her knew what she was talking about.

If you ever look at a picture of someone who has just had an idea, you might notice a drawing of a lightbulb over the person's head. Of course, there is not usually a lightbulb hovering in the air when someone has an idea, but the image of a lightbulb over someone's head has become a sort of symbol for thinking, just as the image of an eye, sadly, has become a symbol for crime and devious behavior rather

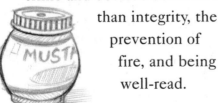

than integrity, the prevention of fire, and being well-read.

As Violet and Quigley climbed back down the slippery slope of the frozen waterfall, their fork-assisted climbing shoes poking into the ice with each step, they looked down and saw, by the last light of the setting sun, the figure of Klaus. He was holding a flashlight over his head to help the two climbers find their way down, but it looked as if he'd just had an idea.

"He must have found a flashlight in the wreckage," Quigley said. "It looks like the one Jacques gave me."

"I hope he found enough information to decode Verbal Fridge Dialogue," Violet said, and tapped the candelabra below her feet. "Be careful here, Quigley. The ice feels thin. We'll have to climb around it."

"The ice has been less solid on our way down," Quigley said.

"That's not surprising," Violet said. "We've poked a great deal of it with forks. By the time False Spring arrives, this whole slope will probably only be half frozen."

"By the time False Spring arrives," Quigley said, "I hope we'll be on our way to the last safe place."

"Me, too," Violet said quietly, and the two climbers said no more until they reached the bottom of the waterfall and walked carefully across the frozen pool along the path Klaus shone with his flashlight.

"I'm so glad you returned in one piece," Klaus said, shining his flashlight in the direction of the dining room remains. "It looked like a very slippery journey. It's getting cold, but if we sit behind the library entrance, we'll be away from much of the wind."

But Violet was so eager to tell her brother who they had found at the top of the peak that she could not wait another moment. "It's Sunny," she said. "Sunny's at the top. It was her who was signaling us."

"Sunny?" Klaus said, his eyes as wide as his smile. "How did she get up there? Is she safe? Why didn't you bring her back?"

"She's safe," Violet said. "She's with Count Olaf, but she's safe."

"Has he harmed her?" Klaus asked.

Violet shook her head. "No," she said. "He's making her do all the cooking and cleaning."

"But she's a baby!" Klaus said.

"Not anymore," Violet said. "We haven't noticed, Klaus, but she's grown up quite a bit. She's really too young to be in charge of all the chores, of course, but sometime, during all the hardship we've been through, she stopped being a baby."

"She's old enough to eavesdrop," Quigley said. "She's already discovered who burned down the V.F.D. headquarters."

"They're two terrible people, a man and a woman, who have quite an aura of menace," Violet said. "Even Count Olaf is a little afraid of them."

"What are they all doing up there?" Klaus asked.

"They're having some sort of villainous

meeting," Quigley said. "We heard them mention something about a recruitment plan, and a large net."

"That doesn't sound pleasant," Klaus said.

"There's more, Klaus," Violet said. "Count Olaf has the Snicket file, and he found out about some secret location—the last safe place where the V.F.D. can gather. That's why Sunny stayed up there. If she overhears where the place is, we'll know where to go to meet up with the rest of the volunteers."

"I hope she manages to find out," Klaus said. "Without that piece of information, all that I've discovered is useless."

"What have you discovered?" Quigley asked.

"I'll show you," Klaus said, and led the way to the ruins of the library, where Violet could see he'd been working. His dark blue notebook was open, and she could see that several pages were filled with notes. Nearby were several half-burnt scraps of paper, stacked underneath a burnt teacup Klaus was using for a paperweight, and all of the contents of the refrigerator were laid out in a careful half circle: the jar of mustard, the container of olives, three jars of jam, and the very fresh dill. The small glass jug, containing one pickle, and the bottle of lemon juice were off to one side. "This is some of the most difficult research I've ever done," Klaus said, sitting down next to his notebook. "Justice Strauss's legal library was confusing, and Aunt Josephine's grammatical library was dull, but the ruined V.F.D. library is a much bigger challenge. Even if I know what book I'm looking for, it may be nothing but ashes."

"Did you find anything about Verbal Fridge Dialogue?" Quigley asked, sitting beside him.

"Not at first," Klaus said. "The scrap of paper that led us to the refrigerator was in a large pile of ashes, and it took awhile to sift through it. But I finally found one page that was probably from the same book." He reached for his notebook and held up his flashlight so he could see the pages. "The page was so delicate," he said, "that

I immediately copied it into my commonplace book. It explains how the whole code works."

"Read it to us," Violet said, and Klaus complied, a word which here means "followed Violet's suggestion and read a very complicated paragraph out loud, explaining it as he went along."

"'Verbal Fridge Dialogue,'" he read, "'is an emergency communication system that avails itself of the more esoteric products in a refrigerator. Volunteers will know such a code is being used by the presence of very fr—'" He looked up from his notebook. "The sentence ends there," he said, "but I assume that 'very fr' is the beginning of 'very fresh dill.' If very fresh dill is in the refrigerator, that means there's a message there, too."

"I understand that part," Violet said, "but what does 'esoteric' mean?"

"In this case," Klaus said, "I think it refers to things that aren't used very much—the things that stay in the refrigerator for a long time."

"Like mustard and jam and things like that," Violet said. "I understand."

"'The receiver of the message should find his or her initials, as noted by one of our poet volunteers, as follows,'" Klaus continued. "And then there's a short poem:

"The darkest of the jams of three
contains within the addressee."

"That's a couplet," Quigley said, "like my sister writes."

"I don't think your sister wrote that particular poem," Violet said. "This code was probably invented before your sister was born."

"That's what I thought," Klaus said, "but it made me wonder who taught Isadora about couplets. They might have been a volunteer."

"She had a poetry teacher when we were young," Quigley said, "but I never met him. I always had cartography class."

"And your mapmaking skills," Violet said,

"led us to the headquarters."

"And your inventing skills," Klaus said, "allowed you to climb up to Mount Fraught."

"And your researching skills are helping us now," Violet said. "It's as if we were being trained for all this, and we didn't even know it."

"I never thought of learning about maps as training," Quigley said. "I just liked it."

"Well, I haven't had much training in poetry," Klaus said, "but the couplet seems to say that inside the darkest jar of jam is the name of the person who's supposed to get the message."

Violet looked down at the three jars of jam. "There's apricot, strawberry, and boysenberry," she said. "Boysenberry's the darkest."

Klaus nodded, and unscrewed the cap from the jar of boysenberry jam. "Look inside," he said, and shined the flashlight so Violet and Quigley could see. Someone had taken a knife and written two letters in the surface of the jam: J and S.

"J.S.," Quigley said. "Jacques Snicket."

"The message can't be for Jacques Snicket," Violet said. "He's dead."

"Maybe whoever wrote this message doesn't know that," Klaus said, and continued to read from the commonplace book. "'If necessary, the dialogue uses a cured, fruit-based calendar for days of the week in order to announce a gathering. Sunday is represented by a lone—' Here it's cut off again, but I think that means that these olives are an encoded way of communicating which day of the week a gathering will take place, with Sunday being one olive, Monday being two, and so on."

"How many olives are in that container?" Quigley asked.

"Five," Klaus said, wrinkling his nose. "I didn't like counting them. Ever since the Squalors fixed us aqueous martinis, the taste of olives hasn't really appealed to me."

"Five olives means Thursday," Violet said.

"Today's Friday," Quigley said. "The gathering of the volunteers is less than a week away."

The two Baudelaires nodded in agreement, and Klaus opened his notebook again. "'Any spice-based condiment,'" he read, "'should have a coded label referring volunteers to encoded poems.'"

"I don't think I understand," Quigley said.

Klaus sighed, and reached for the jar of mustard. "This is where it really gets complicated. Mustard is a spice-based condiment, and according to the code, it should refer us to a poem of some sort."

"How can mustard refer us to a poem?" Violet asked.

Klaus smiled. "I was puzzled for a long time," he said, "but I finally thought to look at the list of ingredients. Listen to this: 'Vinegar, mustard seed, salt, tumeric, the final quatrain of the eleventh stanza of "The Garden of Proserpine," by Algernon Charles Swinburne, and calcium disodium, an allegedly natural preservative.' A quatrain is four lines of a poem, and a stanza is another word for a verse. They hid a reference to a poem in the list of ingredients."

"It's the perfect place to hide something," Violet said. "No one ever reads those lists very carefully. But did you find the poem?"

Klaus frowned, and lifted the teacup. "Under a burnt wooden sign marked 'Poetry,' I found a pile of papers that were burned practically beyond recognition," he said, "but here's the one surviving scrap, and it's the last quatrain of the eleventh stanza of 'The Garden of Proserpine,' by Algernon Charles Swinburne."

"That's convenient," Quigley said.

"A little *too* convenient," Klaus said. "The entire library was destroyed, and the one poem that survived is the one we need. It can't be a coincidence." He held out the scrap of paper so Violet and Quigley could see it. "It's as if someone knew we'd be looking for this."

"What does the quatrain say?" Violet asked.

"It's not very cheerful," Klaus said, and tilted the flashlight so he could read it:

"That no life lives forever;
That dead men rise up never;
That even the weariest river
Winds somewhere safe to sea."

The children shivered, and moved so they were sitting even closer together on the ground. It had grown darker, and Klaus's flashlight was pratically the only thing they could see. If you have ever found yourself sitting in darkness with a flashlight, you may have experienced the feeling that something is lurking just beyond the circle of light that a flashlight makes, and reading a poem about dead men is not a good way to make yourself feel better.

"I wish Isadora were here," Quigley said. "She could tell us what that poem means."

"*Even the weariest river winds somewhere safe to sea,*" Violet repeated. "Do you think that refers to the last safe place?"

"I don't know," Klaus said. "I couldn't find

anything else that would help us."

"What about the lemon juice?" Violet asked. "And the pickle?"

Klaus shook his head, although his sister could scarcely see him in the dark. "There might be more to the message," he said, "but it's all gone up in smoke. I couldn't find anything more in the library that seemed helpful."

Violet took the scrap of paper from her brother and looked at the quatrain. "There's something very faint here," she said. "Something written in pencil, but it's too faint to read."

Quigley reached into his backpack. "I forgot we have two flashlights," he said, and shone a second light onto the paper. Sure enough, there was one word, written very faintly in pencil beside the last four lines of the poem's eleventh stanza. Violet, Klaus, and Quigley leaned in as far as they could to see what it was. The night winds rustled the fragile paper, and made the children shiver, shaking the flashlights, but at last the light shone on the quatrain and they could see what words were there.

"Sugar bowl," they said in unison, and looked at one another.

"What could that mean?" Klaus asked.

Violet sighed. "When we were hiding underneath the car," she said to Quigley, "one of those villains said something about searching for a sugar bowl, remember?"

Quigley nodded, and took out his purple notebook. "Jacques Snicket mentioned a sugar bowl once," he said, "when we were in Dr. Montgomery's library. He said it was very important to find it. I wrote it down on the top of a page in my commonplace book, so I could add any information I learned about its whereabouts." He held up the page so the two Baudelaires could see that it was blank. "I never learned anything more," he said.

Klaus sighed. "It seems that the more we learn, the more mysteries we find. We reached V.F.D. headquarters and decoded a message, and all we know is that there's one last safe place, and volunteers are gathering there on Thursday."

"That might be enough," Violet said, "if Sunny finds out where the safe place is."

"But how are we going to get Sunny away from Count Olaf?" Klaus asked.

"With your fork-assisted climbing shoes," Quigley said. "We can climb up there again, and sneak away with Sunny."

Violet shook her head. "The moment they noticed Sunny was gone," she said, "they would find us. From Mount Fraught, they can see everything and everyone for miles and miles, and we're hopelessly outnumbered."

"That's true," Quigley admitted. "There are ten villains up there, and only four of us. Then how are we going to rescue her?"

"Olaf has someone we love," Klaus said thoughtfully. "If we had something he loves, we could trade it for Sunny's return. What does Count Olaf love?"

"Money," Violet said.

"Fire," Quigley said.

"We don't have any money," Klaus said, "and Olaf won't trade Sunny for a fire. There must be something he really loves—something that makes him happy, and would make him very unhappy if it were taken away."

Violet and Quigley looked at one another and smiled. "Count Olaf loves Esmé Squalor," Violet said. "If we were holding Esmé prisoner, we could arrange a trade."

"That's true," Klaus said, "but we're not holding Esmé prisoner."

"We could take her prisoner," Quigley said, and everyone was quiet. Taking someone prisoner, of course, is a villainous thing to do, and when you think of doing a villainous thing— even if you have a very good reason for thinking of doing it—it can make you feel like a villain, too. Lately, the Baudelaires had been doing things like wearing disguises and helping burn down a carnival, and were beginning to feel more and more like villains themselves. But

Violet and Klaus had never done anything as villainous as taking somebody prisoner, and as
they looked at Quigley they could tell that he
felt just as uncomfortable, sitting in the dark
and thinking up a villainous plan.

"How would we do it?" Klaus asked quietly.

"We could lure her to us," Violet said, "and
trap her."

Quigley wrote something down in his commonplace book. "We could use the Verdant
Flammable Devices," he said. "Esmé thinks
they're cigarettes, and she thinks cigarettes are
in. If we lit some of them, she might smell the
smoke and come down here."

"But then what?" Klaus asked.

Violet shivered in the cold, and reached
into her pocket. Her fingers bumped up
against the large bread knife, which she had
almost forgotten was there, and then found
what she was looking for. She took the ribbon
out of her pocket and tied her hair up, to keep it
out of her eyes. The eldest Baudelaire could

scarcely believe she was using her inventing skills to think up a trap. "The easiest trap to build," she said, "is a pit. We could dig a deep hole, and cover it up with some of this half-burned wood so Esmé couldn't see it. The wood has been weakened by the fire, so when she steps on it . . ."

Violet did not finish her sentence, but by the glow of the flashlights, she could see that Klaus and Quigley were both nodding. "Hunters have used traps like that for centuries," Klaus said, "to capture wild animals."

"That doesn't make me feel any better," Violet said.

"How could we dig such a pit?" Quigley said.

"Well," Violet said, "we don't really have any tools, so we probably have to use our hands. As the pit got deeper, we'd have to use something to carry the dirt away."

"I still have that pitcher," Klaus said.

"And we'd need a way to make sure that we wouldn't get trapped ourselves," Violet said.

"I have a rope," Quigley said, "in my back-pack. We could tie one end to the archway, and use it to climb out."

Violet reached her hand down to the ground. The dirt was very cold, but quite loose, and she saw that they could dig a pit without too much trouble. "Is this the right thing to do?" Violet asked. "Do you think this is what our parents would do?"

"Our parents aren't here," Klaus said. "They might have been here once, but they're not here now."

The children were quiet again, and tried to think as best they could in the cold and the dark. Deciding on the right thing to do in a situation is a bit like deciding on the right thing to wear to a party. It is easy to decide on what is wrong to wear to a party, such as deep-sea diving equipment or a pair of large pillows, but deciding what is right is much trickier. It might seem right to wear a navy blue suit, for instance, but when you arrive there could be several other people wearing the same thing, and you could end up being hand-cuffed due to a case of mistaken identity. It might seem right to wear your favorite pair of shoes, but there could be a sudden flood at the party, and your shoes would be ruined. And it might seem right to wear a suit of armor to the party, but there could be several other people wearing the same thing, and you could end up being caught in a flood due to a case of mistaken identity, and find yourself drifting out to sea wishing that you were wearing deep-sea diving equipment after all. The truth is that you can never be sure if you have decided on the right thing until the party is over, and by then it is too late to go back and change your mind, which is why the world is filled with people doing terrible things and wearing ugly clothing, and so few volunteers who are able to stop them.

"I don't know if it's the right thing to do," Violet said, "but Count Olaf captured Sunny, and we might have to capture someone our-selves, in order to stop him."

Klaus nodded solemnly. "We'll fight fire," he said, "with fire."

"Then we'd better get started," Quigley said, and stood up. "When the sun rises, we can light the Verdant Flammable Devices with the mirror again, like we did when we were signaling Sunny."

"If we want the pit to be ready by dawn," Violet said, "we'll have to dig all night."

"Where shall we put the pit?" Klaus asked.

"In front of the entrance," Violet decided. "Then we can hide behind the arch when Esmé approaches."

"How will we know when she's fallen in," Quigley asked, "if we can't see her?"

"We'll hear it," Violet replied. "We'll hear the breaking of the wood, and Esmé might scream."

Klaus shuddered. "That's not going to be a pleasant sound."

"We're not in a pleasant situation," Violet said, and the eldest Baudelaire was right. It was not pleasant to kneel down in front of the ruined library entrance, and dig through the ashes and dirt with their bare hands by the light of two flash-lights, as all four drafts of the valley blew around them. It was not pleasant for Violet and her brother to carry the dirt away in the pitcher, while Quigley tied his rope to the iron archway, so they could climb in and out as the pit grew bigger and deeper, like an enormous dark mouth opening wider and wider to swallow them whole. It was not even pleasant to pause and eat a carrot to keep up their energy, or to gaze at the shiny white shape of the frozen waterfall as it glinted in the moonlight, imagining Esmé Squalor, lured by the smoke of the Verdant Flammable Devices, approaching the ruined headquarters to become their prisoner. But the least pleasant part of the situation wasn't the cold dirt, or the freezing winds, or even their own exhaustion as it grew later and later and the children dug deeper and deeper. The least pleasant part was the idea, shared by the two Baudelaires and their new friend, that they might be doing a villainous thing.

The siblings were not sure if digging a deep pit to trap someone, in order to trade prisoners with a villain, was something that their parents or any other volunteers would do, but with so many of the V.F.D. secrets lost in the ashes, it was impossible to know for sure, and this uncertainty haunted them with every pitcherful of dirt, and every climb up the rope, and every piece of weakened wood they laid on top of the pit to hide it from view.

As the first rays of the morning sun appeared on the misty horizon, the elder Baudelaires gazed up at the waterfall. At the summit of the Mortmain Mountains, they knew, was a group of villains, from whom Sunny was hopefully learning the location of the last safe place. But as Violet and Klaus lowered their gaze to their own handiwork, and looked at the dark, deep pit Quigley had helped them dig, they could not help wondering if there were also a group of villains at the bottom of the slippery slope. As they looked at the villainous thing they had made, the three volunteers could not help wondering if they were villains, too, and this was the least pleasant feeling in the world.

Not too long ago, in the
Swedish city of Stock-
holm, a group of bank
robbers took a few
prisoners during
the course of
their work.
For several
days, the

bank robbers and the prisoners lived together in close proximity, a word which here means "while the police gathered outside and eventually managed to arrest the robbers and take them to jail." When the prisoners were finally freed, however, the authorities discovered that they had become friends with the bank robbers, and since that time the expression "Stockholm Syndrome" has been used to describe a situation in which someone becomes friendly with the people who are holding them prisoner.

There is another expression, however, which describes a situation that is far more common, when a prisoner does not become friends with such people, but instead regards them as villains, and despises them more and more with each passing moment, waiting desperately for an opportunity to escape. The expression is "Mount Fraught Syndrome," and Sunny Baudelaire was experiencing it as she stood at the top of Mount Fraught, gazing down at the frozen waterfall and thinking about her circumstances.

The young girl had spent another sleepless night in the covered casserole dish, after washing the salmon out of it with a few handfuls of melted snow. It was chilly, of course, with the winds of the Mortmain Mountains blowing through the holes in the lid, and it was painful, because once again her teeth were chattering in the cold and giving her tiny cuts on her lips, but there was another reason Sunny did not sleep well, which is that she was frustrated. Despite her best spying attempts, the youngest Baudelaire had been unable to eavesdrop on the villains' conversation and learn the location of the last safe place where V.F.D. would be gathering, or learn any more about the dreadful recruitment scheme planned by the man with a beard but no hair and the woman with hair but no beard. When the troupe gathered around the flat rock for dinner, they discussed these things, but every time Sunny tried to get close enough to hear what they were saying, they glared at her and quickly changed the subject. It seemed to

Sunny that the only thing she had accomplished all evening was preparing a meal that the troupe enjoyed. When she had presented her platter of False Spring Rolls, no one had complained, and every single villainous person had taken second helpings.

But something crucial had escaped the attention of Count Olaf and his comrades during the meal, and for that Sunny was very grateful. As she had told her siblings, the youngest Baudelaire had prepared an assortment of vegetables wrapped in spinach leaves, in honor of False Spring. Her recipe had required the bag of mushrooms, the can of water chestnuts, and the frozen hunk of spinach, which she had thawed by holding it underneath her shirt, as she had when preparing toast tartar. But Sunny had decided at the last minute that she would not use the enormous eggplant. When Violet mentioned that the eggplant must weigh as much as Sunny did, the youngest Baudelaire had an idea, and rather than chopping the eggplant into small strips with her teeth, she hid it behind the flat tire of Count Olaf's car, and now, as the sun rose and the group of villains began their usual morning bickering, she was retrieving the eggplant and rolling it to the casserole dish. As she rolled it past the automobile, Sunny looked down at the frozen waterfall, which was looking less and less frozen in the morning sun. She knew her siblings were at the bottom with Quigley, and although she couldn't see them, it made her feel better knowing they were relatively nearby and that, if her plan worked out, she would soon be joining them.

"What are you doing, baby?" Sunny had just slipped the eggplant under the cover of the casserole dish when she heard the voice of one of Olaf's comrades. The two white-faced women were standing just outside their tent and stretching in the morning sun.

"Aubergine," Sunny replied, which meant "I've concocted a plan involving this eggplant, and it doesn't matter if I tell you about it because you never understand a single word I say."

"More babytalk," said the other white-faced woman with a sigh. "I'm beginning to think that Sunny is only a helpless baby, and not a spy."

"Goo goo ga—" Sunny began, but the flap of Count Olaf's tent opened before she could utter the last "ga." The villain and his girlfriend stood in the morning sun, and it was clear that they expected the new day—Saturday—to be an important one, because they were dressed for the occasion, a phrase which here means "wearing such strange clothing that the youngest Baudelaire was too surprised to say the final 'ga' she had been planning." Amazingly, it appeared that Count Olaf had washed his face, and he was wearing a brand-new suit made out of material that at first seemed to be covered in tiny polka dots. But when Sunny took a closer look, she saw that each dot was a small eye, matching Olaf's tattoo and the V.F.D. insignia and all of the other eyes that had plagued the Baudelaires since that terrible day on the beach, so that looking at Count Olaf in his new suit felt like looking at a crowd of villains, all staring at Sunny Baudelaire. But no matter how unnerving Olaf's fashion choice was, Esmé Squalor's outfit was worse to behold. Sunny could not remember when she had ever seen a dress so enormous, and was surprised that such an article of clothing could have fit in the tent and still leave room for villains to sleep. The dress was made of layers upon layers of shiny cloth, in different shades of yellow, orange, and red, all cut in fierce triangular shapes so that each layer seemed to cut into the next, and rising from the shoulders of the dress were enormous piles of black lace, sticking up into the air in strange curves. For a moment, the dress was so huge and odd that Sunny could not imagine why anyone would wear it, but as the wicked girlfriend stepped farther out of the tent, it became horribly clear. Esmé Squalor was dressed to look like an enormous fire.

"What a wonderful morning!" Count Olaf

crowed. "Just think, by the end of the day I'll have more new members of my troupe than ever before!"

"And we'll need them," Esmé agreed. "We're all going to have to work together for the greater good—burning down the last safe place!"

"Just the idea of the Hotel Denouement in flames makes me so excited, I'm going to open a bottle of wine!" Count Olaf announced, and Sunny covered her mouth with her hands so the villains would not hear her gasp. The Hotel Denouement, she realized, must be the last safe place for volunteers to gather, and Olaf was so excited that he had uttered the name inadvertently, a word which here means "where the youngest Baudelaire could hear it."

"The idea of all those eagles filling the sky makes me so excited, I'm going to smoke one of those in green cigarettes!" Esmé announced, and then frowned. "Except I don't have one. Drat."

"Beg your pardon, your Esméship," said one of the white-faced women, "but I see some of that green smoke down at the bottom of the waterfall."

"Really?" Esmé asked eagerly, and looked in the direction Olaf's employee was pointing. Sunny looked, too, and saw a familiar plume of green smoke at the very bottom of the slope, getting bigger and bigger as the sun continued to rise. The youngest Baudelaire wondered why her siblings were signaling her, and what they were trying to say.

"That's strange," Olaf said. "You'd think there'd be nothing left of the headquarters to burn."

"Look how much smoke there is," Esmé said greedily. "There must be a whole pack of cigarettes down there. This day is getting even better!"

Count Olaf smiled, and then looked away from the waterfall and noticed Sunny for the first time. "I'll have the baby go down and get them for you," Count Olaf said.

"Yessir!" Sunny said eagerly.

"The baby would probably steal all the cigarettes for herself," Esmé said, glaring at the young girl. "I'll go."

"But climbing down there will take hours," Olaf said. "Don't you want to be here for the recruitment scheme? I just love springing traps on people."

"Me, too," Esmé agreed, "but don't worry, Olaf. I'll be back in moments. I'm not going to climb. I'll take one of the toboggans and sled down the waterfall before anyone else even notices I'm gone."

"Drat!" Sunny couldn't help saying. She meant something along the lines of, "That is exactly what I was planning on doing," but once again no one understood.

"Shut up, toothy," Esmé said, "and get out of my way." She flounced past the youngest Baudelaire, and Sunny realized that there was something sewn to the bottom of the dress that made it make a crackling noise as she walked, so that the wicked girlfriend sounded as much like a fire as she looked like one. Blowing a kiss to Count Olaf, she grabbed the toboggan belonging to sinister villains.

"I'll be right back, darling," Esmé said. "Tell that baby to take a nap so she won't see what we're up to."

"Esmé's right," Olaf said, giving Sunny a cruel smile. "Get in the casserole dish. You're such an ugly, helpless creature, I can scarcely stand to look at you."

"You said it, handsome," Esmé said, and chuckled meanly as she sat at the top of the waterfall. The two white-faced women scurried to help, and gave the toboggan a big push as Sunny did as she was told, and disappeared from Olaf's sight.

As you may imagine, the sight of a grown woman in an enormous flame-imitating dress tobogganing down from the source of the Stricken Stream to the two tributaries and the half-frozen pool at the bottom of the waterfall is not the sort of thing to pass unnoticed, even from far away. Violet was the first to see the colorful blur heading quickly down the slope, and she lowered Colette's hand mirror, which she had used once again to catch the rays of the rising sun and reflect them onto the Verdant Flammable Devices, which she had put in a pile in front of the pit. Wrinkling her nose from the bitter smell of the smoke, she turned to Klaus and Quigley, who were putting one last piece of weakened wood across the pit, so their trap would be hidden from view.

"Look," Violet said, and pointed to the descending shape.

"Do you think it's Esmé?" Klaus asked.

Violet squinted up at the tobogganing figure. "I think so," she said. "Nobody but Esmé Squalor would wear an outfit like that."

"We'd better hide behind the archway," Quigley said, "before she spots us."

The two Baudelaires nodded in agreement, and walked carefully to the library entrance, making sure to step around the hole they had dug.

"I'm happy that we can't see the pit any-more," Klaus said. "Looking into that blackness reminded me of that terrible passageway at 667 Dark Avenue."

"First Esmé trapped your siblings there," Violet said to Quigley, "and then she trapped us."

"And now we're fighting fire with fire, and trapping her," Quigley said uncomfortably.

"It's best not to think about it," Violet said, although she had not stopped thinking about the trap since the first handful of ashes and earth. "Soon we'll have Sunny back, and that's what's important."

"Maybe this is important, too," Klaus said, and pointed up at the archway. "I never noticed it until now."

Violet and Quigley looked up to see what he was referring to, and saw four tiny words etched over their heads, right underneath the large let-ters spelling "V.F.D. Library."

"'The world is quiet here,'" Quigley read. "What do you think it means?"

"It looks like a motto," Klaus said. "At Prufrock Preparatory School, they had a motto carved near the entrance, so everyone would remember it when they entered the academy."

Violet shook her head. "That's not what I'm thinking of," she said. "I'm remembering something about that phrase, but just barely."

"The world certainly feels quiet around here," Klaus said. "We haven't heard a single snow gnat since we arrived."

"The smell of smoke scares them away, remember?" Quigley asked.

"Of course," Klaus said, and peered around the archway to check on Esmé's progress. The colorful blur was about halfway down the waterfall, heading straight for the trap they had built. "There's been so much smoke here at headquarters, the gnats might never come back."

"Without snow gnats," Quigley said, "the salmon of the Stricken Stream will go hungry. They feed on snow gnats." He reached into his pocket and opened his commonplace book.

"And without salmon," he said, "the Mortmain Mountain eagles will go hungry. The destruction of V.F.D. headquarters has caused even more damage than I thought."

Klaus nodded in agreement. "When we were walking along the Stricken Stream," he said, "the fish were coughing from all the ashes in the water. Remember, Violet?"

He turned to his sister, but Violet was only half listening. She was still gazing at the words on the archway, and trying to remember where she heard them before. "I can just hear those words," she said. *The world is quiet here.* "She closed her eyes. "I think it was a very long time ago, before you were born, Klaus."

"Maybe someone said them to you," Quigley said.

Violet tried to remember as far back as she could, but everything seemed as misty as it did in the mountains. She could see the face of her mother, and her father standing behind her, wearing a suit as black as the ashes of V.F.D.

headquarters. Their mouths were open, but Violet could not remember what they were saying. No matter how hard she tried, the memory was as silent as the grave. "Nobody said them to me," she said finally. "Someone *sang* them. I think my parents sang the words 'the world is quiet here' a long time ago, but I don't know why." She opened her eyes and faced her brother and her friend. "I think we might be doing the wrong thing," she said.

"But we agreed," Quigley said, "to fight fire with fire."

Violet nodded, and stuck her hands in her pocket, bumping up against the bread knife again. She thought of the darkness of the pit, and the scream Esmé would make as she fell into it. "I know we agreed," Violet said, "but if V.F.D. really stands for Volunteer Fire Department, then they're an organization that stops fire. If everyone fought fire with fire, the entire world would go up in smoke."

"I see what you mean," Quigley said. "If the V.F.D. motto is 'The world is quiet here,' we ought to be doing something less noisy and violent than trapping someone, no matter how wicked they are."

"When I was looking into the pit," Klaus said quietly, "I was remembering something I read in a book by a famous philosopher. He said, 'Whoever fights monsters should see to it that in the process he does not become a monster. And when you look long into an abyss, the abyss also looks into you.'" Klaus looked at his sister, and then at the sight of Esmé approaching, and then at the weakened wood that the three children had placed on the ground. "'Abyss' is a fancy word for 'pit,'" he said. "We built an abyss for Esmé to fall into. That's something a monster might do."

Quigley was copying Klaus's words into his commonplace book. "What happened to that philosopher?" he asked.

"He's dead," Klaus replied. "I think you're right, Violet. We don't want to be as villainous and monstrous as Count Olaf."

"But what are we going to do?" Quigley asked. "Sunny is still Olaf's prisoner, and Esmé will be here at any moment. If we don't think of the right thing right now, it'll be too late."

As soon as the triplet finished his sentence, however, the three children heard something that made them realize it might already be too late. From behind the archway, Violet, Klaus, and Quigley heard a rough, scraping sound as the toboggan reached the bottom of the waterfall and slid to a halt, and then a triumphant giggle from the mouth of Esmé Squalor. The three volunteers peeked around the archway and saw the treacherous girlfriend step off the toboggan with a greedy smile on her face. But when Esmé adjusted her enormous flame-imitating dress and took a step toward the smoking Verdant Flammable Devices, Violet was not looking at her any more. Violet was looking down at the ground, just a few steps from where she was standing. Three dark, round masks were sitting in a pile, where Violet, Klaus, and Quigley had left them upon arriving at the ruins of headquarters. They had assumed that they would not need them again, but the eldest Baudelaire realized they had been wrong. As Esmé took another step closer to the trap, Violet dashed over to the masks, put one on and stepped out of her hiding place as her brother and her friend looked on.

"Stop, Esmé!" she cried. "It's a trap!"

Esmé stopped in her tracks and gave Violet a curious look. "Who are you?" she asked. "You shouldn't sneak up on people like that. It's a villainous thing to do."

"I'm a volunteer," Violet said.

Esmé's mouth, heavy with orange lipstick that matched her dress, curled into a sneer. "There are no volunteers here," she said. "The entire headquarters are destroyed!"

Klaus was the next to grab a mask and confront Olaf's treacherous romantic companion.

"Our headquarters might be destroyed," he said, "but the V.F.D. is as strong as ever!"

Esmé frowned at the two siblings as if she couldn't decide whether to be frightened or not. "You may be strong," she said nervously, "but you're also very short." Her dress crackled as she started to take another step toward the pit. "When I get my hands on you—"

"No!" Quigley cried, and stepped out from the arch wearing his mask, taking care not to fall into his own trap. "Don't come any closer, Esmé. If you take another step, you'll fall into our trap."

"You're making that up," Esmé said, but she did not move any closer. "You're trying to keep all the cigarettes for yourself."

"They're not cigarettes," Klaus said, "and we're not liars. Underneath the wood you're about to step on is a very deep pit."

Esmé looked at them suspiciously. Gingerly—a word which here means "without falling into a very deep hole"—she leaned down and moved a piece of wood aside, and stared down into the trap the children had built. "Well, well, well," she said. "You *did* build a trap. I never would have fallen for it, of course, but I must admit you dug quite a pit."

"We wanted to trap you," Violet said, "so we could trade you for the safe return of Sunny Baudelaire. But—"

"But you didn't have the courage to go through with it," Esmé said with a mocking smile. "You volunteers are never brave enough to do something for the greater good."

"Throwing people into pits isn't the greater good!" Quigley cried. "It's villainous treachery!"

"If you weren't such an idiot," Esmé said, "you'd realize that those things are more or less the same."

"He is not an idiot," Violet said fiercely. She knew, of course, that it was not worthwhile to get upset over insults from such a ridiculous person, but she liked Quigley too much to hear him called names. "He led us here to the headquarters using a map he drew himself."

"He's very well-read," Klaus said.

At Klaus's words, Esmé threw back her head and laughed, shaking the crackling layers of her enormous dress. *"Well-read!"* she repeated in a particularly nasty tone of voice. "Being well-read won't help you in this world. Many years ago, I was supposed to waste my entire summer reading *Anna Karenina*, but I knew that silly book would never help me, so I threw it into the fireplace." She reached down and picked up a few more pieces of wood, which she tossed aside with a snicker. "Look at your precious headquarters, volunteers! It's as ruined as my book. And look at *me*! I'm beautiful, fashionable, and I smoke cigarettes!" She laughed again, and pointed at the children with a scornful finger. "If you didn't spend all your time with your heads stuck in books, you'd have that precious baby back."

"We're going to get her back," Violet said firmly.

"Really?" Esmé said mockingly. "And how do you propose to do that?"

"I'm going to talk to Count Olaf," Violet said, "and he's going to give her back to me."

Esmé threw back her head and started to laugh, but not with as much enthusiasm as before. "What do you mean?" she said.

"Just what I said," Violet said.

"Hmmm," Esmé said suspiciously. "Let me think for a moment." The evil girlfriend began to pace back and forth on the frozen pond, her enormous dress crackling with every step.

Klaus leaned in to whisper to his sister. "What are you doing?" he asked. "Do you honestly think that we can get Sunny back from Count Olaf with a simple conversation?"

"I don't know," Violet whispered back, "but it's better than luring someone into a trap."

"It was wrong to dig that pit," Quigley agreed, "but I'm not sure that walking straight into Olaf's clutches is the right thing to do, either."

"It'll take a while to reach Mount Fraught again," Violet said. "We'll think of something during the climb."

"I hope so," Klaus said, "but if we can't think of something—"

Klaus did not get a chance to say what might happen if they couldn't think of something, because Esmé clapped her hands together to get the children's attention.

"If you really want to talk to my boyfriend," she said, "I suppose I can take you to where he is. If you weren't so stupid, you'd know that he's very nearby."

"We know where he is, Esmé," Klaus said. "He's at the top of the waterfall, at the source of the Stricken Stream."

"Then I suppose you know how we can get there," Esmé said, and looked a little foolish. "The toboggan doesn't go uphill, so I actually have no idea how we can reach the peak."

"She will invent a way," Quigley said, pointing at Violet.

Violet smiled at her friend, grateful for his support, and closed her eyes underneath her mask. Once more, she was thinking of something she had heard sung to her, when she was a very little girl. She had already thought of the way that the three children could take Esmé with them when they ascended the hill, but thinking of their journey made her think of a song she had not thought of for many years. Perhaps when you were very young, someone sang this song to you, perhaps to lull you to sleep, or to entertain you on a long car trip, or in order to teach you a secret code. The song is called "The Itsy Bitsy Spider," and it is one of the saddest songs ever composed. It tells the story of a small spider who is trying to climb up a water spout, but every time its climb is half over, there is a great burst of water, either due to rain or somebody turning the spout on, and at the end of the song, the spider has decided to try one more time, and will likely be washed away once again.

Violet Baudelaire could not help feeling like this poor spider as she ascended the waterfall for the last time, with Quigley and Klaus beside her and Esmé Squalor on her toboggan behind them. After attaching the last two forks to Klaus's shoes, she had told her companions to tie the leather straps of the toboggan around their waists, so they could drag the villainous girlfriend behind them as they climbed. It was exhausting to approach the peak of Mount Fraught in this manner, particularly after staying up all night digging a pit, and it seemed like they might get washed back down by the dripping water of the Stricken Stream, like the spider Violet had heard about when she was a little girl. The ice on the slope was weakening, after two fork-assisted climbs, a toboggan ride, and the increasing temperatures of False Spring, and with each step of Violet's invention, the ice would shift slightly. It was clear that the slippery slope was almost as exhausted as they were, and soon the ice would vanish completely.

"Mush!" Esmé called from the toboggan. She was using an expression that arctic explorers shouted to their sled dogs, and it certainly did not make the journey any easier.

"I wish she'd stop saying that," Violet murmured from behind her mask. She tapped the candelabra on the ice ahead of her, and a small piece detached from the waterfall and fell to the ruins of headquarters. She watched it disappear below her and sighed. She would never see the V.F.D. headquarters in all its glory. None of the Baudelaires would. Violet would never know how it felt to cook in the kitchen and gaze at the two tributaries of the Stricken Stream, while chatting with the other volunteers. Klaus would never know how it felt to relax in the library and learn all of the secrets of V.F.D. in the comfort of one of the library's chairs, with his feet up on one of the matching V.F.D. footstools. Sunny would never operate the projector in the movie room, or practice the art of the fake mustache in the disguise center, or sit in the parlor at tea time and eat the almond cookies made from my grandmother's recipe. Violet would never study chemical composition in one of the six laboratories, and Klaus would never use the balance beams at the gymnasium, and Sunny would never stand behind the counter at the ice cream shop and prepare butterscotch sundaes for the swimming coaches when it was her turn. And none of the Baudelaires would ever meet some of the organization's most beloved volunteers, including the mechanical instructor C. M. Kornbluth, and Dr. Isaac Anwhistle, whom everyone called Ike, and the brave volunteer who tossed the sugar bowl out the kitchen window so it would not be destroyed in the blaze, and watched it float away on one of the tributaries of the Stricken Stream. The Baudelaires would never do any of these things, any more than I will ever see my beloved Beatrice again, or retrieve my pickle from the refrigerator in which I left it, and return it to its rightful place in an important coded sandwich. Violet, of course, was not aware of everything she would never do, but as she gazed down at the vast, ashen remains of the headquarters, she felt as if her whole journey in the Mortmain Mountains had been as useless as the journey of a tiny arachnid in a song she had never liked to hear.

"Mush!" Esmé cried again, with a cruel chuckle.

"Please stop saying that, Esmé," Violet called down impatiently. "That *mush* nonsense is slowing our climb."

"A slow climb might be to our advantage," Klaus murmured to his sister. "The longer it takes us to reach the summit, the longer we have to think up what we're going to say to Count Olaf."

"We could tell him that he's surrounded," Quigley said, "and that there are volunteers everywhere ready to arrest him if he doesn't let Sunny go free."

Violet shook her mask. "He won't believe that," she said, sticking a fork-assisted shoe into the waterfall. "He can see everything and everyone from Mount Fraught. He'll know we're the only volunteers in the area."

"There must be something we can do," Klaus said. "We didn't make this journey into the mountains for nothing."

"Of course not," Quigley said. "We found each other, and we solved some of the mysteries that were haunting us."

"Will that be enough," Violet asked, "to defeat all those villains on the peak?"

Violet's question was a difficult one, and neither Klaus nor Quigley had the answer, and so rather than hazard a guess—a phrase which here means "continue to expend their energy by discussing the matter"—they decided to hazard their climb, a phrase which here means "continue their difficult journey in silence, until they arrived at last at the source of the Stricken Stream." Hoisting themselves up onto the flat peak, they sat on the edge and pulled the leather straps as hard as they could. It was such a difficult task to drag Esmé Squalor and the toboggan over the edge of the slope and onto Mount Fraught that the children did not notice who was nearby until they heard a familiar scratchy voice right behind them.

"Who goes there?" Count Olaf demanded.

Breathless from the climb, the three children turned around to see the villain standing with his two sinister cohorts near his long, black automobile, glaring suspiciously at the masked volunteers.

"We thought you'd get here by taking the path," said the man with a beard but no hair, "not by climbing up the waterfall."

"No, no, no," Esmé said quickly. "These aren't the people we're expecting. These are some volunteers I found at headquarters."

"Volunteers?" said the woman with hair but no beard, but her voice did not sound as deep as it usually did. The villains gave the children the same confused frown they had seen from Esmé, as if they were unsure whether to be scared or scornful, and the hook-handed man, the two white-faced women, and the three former carnival employees gathered around to see what had made their villainous boss fall silent. Although they were exhausted, the two Baudelaires hurriedly untied the straps of the toboggan from their waists and stood with Quigley to face their enemies. The orphans were very scared, of course, but they found that with their faces concealed they could speak their minds, a phrase which here means "confront Count Olaf and his companions as if they weren't one bit frightened."

"We built a trap to capture your girlfriend, Olaf," Violet said, "but we didn't want to become a monster like you."

"They're idiotic *liars*!" Esmé cried. "I found them hogging the cigarettes, so I captured them myself and made them drag me up the waterfall like sled dogs."

The middle Baudelaire ignored the wicked girlfriend's nonsense. "We're here for Sunny Baudelaire," Klaus said, "and we're not leaving without her."

Count Olaf frowned, and peered at them with his shiny, shiny eyes as if he were trying to see through their masks. "And what makes you

so certain," he said, "that I'll give you my prisoner just because you say so?"

Violet thought furiously, looking around at
her surroundings for anything that might give
her an idea of what to do. Count Olaf clearly
believed that the three masked people in front
of him were members of V.F.D., and she felt that
if she could just find the right words to say, she
could defeat him without becoming as villainous as her enemies. But she could not find the
words, and neither could her brother nor her
friend, who stood beside her in silence. The
winds of the Mortmain Mountains blew against
them, and Violet stuck her hands in her pockets, bumping one finger against the long bread
knife. She began to think that perhaps trapping
Esmé had been the right thing to do after all.
Count Olaf's frown began to fade, and his
mouth started to curl upward in a triumphant
smile, but just as he opened his mouth to
speak, Violet saw two things that gave her hope

once more. The first was the sight of two note-books, one a deep shade of purple and the other dark blue, sticking out of the pockets of her companions—commonplace books, where Klaus and Quigley had written down all of the information they had found in the ruined library of V.F.D. headquarters. And the other was a collection of dishes spread out on the flat rock that Olaf's troupe had been using for a table. Sunny had been forced to wash these dishes, using handfuls of melted snow, and she had laid them out to dry in the sunshine of False Spring. Violet could see a stack of plates, each emblazoned with the familiar image of an eye, as well as a row of teacups and a small pitcher for cream. But there was something missing from the tea set, and it made Violet smile behind her mask as she turned to face Count Olaf again.

"You will give us Sunny," she said, "because we know where the sugar bowl is."

Count Olaf gasped, and raised his one eyebrow very high as he gazed at the two Baudelaires and their companion, his eyes shinier than they had ever seen them. *"Where is it?"* he said, in a terrible, wheezing whisper. *"Give it to me!"*

Violet shook her head, grateful that her face was still hidden behind a mask. "Not until you give us Sunny Baudelaire," she said.

"Never!" the villain replied. "Without that big-toothed brat, I'll never capture the Baudelaire fortune. You give me the sugar bowl this instant, or I'll throw all of you off this mountain!"

"If you throw us off the mountain," Klaus said, "you'll never know where the sugar bowl

is." He did not add, of course, that the Baudelaires had no idea where the sugar bowl was, or
why in the world it was so important.

Esmé Squalor took a sinister step toward her
boyfriend, her flame-imitating dress crackling
against the cold ground. "We must have that
sugar bowl," she snarled. "Let the baby go. We'll
cook up another scheme to steal the fortune."

"But stealing the fortune is the greater good,"
Count Olaf said. "We can't let the baby go."

"Getting the sugar bowl is the greater
good," Esmé said, with a frown.

"Stealing the fortune," Olaf insisted.

"Getting the sugar bowl," Esmé replied.

"Fortune!"

"Sugar bowl!"

"Fortune!"

"Sugar bowl!"

"That's enough!" ordered the man with a
beard but no hair. "Our recruitment scheme is
about to be put into action. We can't have you
arguing all day long."

"We wouldn't have argued all day long," Count Olaf said timidly. "After a few hours—"

"We said *that's enough*!" ordered the woman with hair but no beard. "Bring the baby over here!"

"Bring the baby at once!" Count Olaf ordered the two white-faced women. "She's napping in her casserole dish."

The two white-faced women sighed, but hurried over to the casserole dish and lifted it together, as if they were cooks removing something from the oven instead of villainous employees bringing over a prisoner, while the two sinister visitors reached down the necks of their shirts and retrieved something that was hanging around their necks. Violet and Klaus were surprised to see two shiny silver whistles, like the one Count Olaf had used as part of his disguise at Prufrock Preparatory School, when he was pretending to be a coach.

"Watch this, volunteers," said the sinister man in his hoarse voice, and the two mysterious villains blew their whistles. Instantly, the children heard an enormous rustling sound over their heads, as if the Mortmain Mountain winds were as frightened as the youngsters, and it suddenly grew very dim, as if the morning sun had also put on a mask. But when they looked up, Violet, Klaus, and Quigley saw that the reason for the noisy sky and the fading light was perhaps more strange than frightened winds and a masked sun.

The sky above Mount Fraught was swarming with eagles. There were hundreds and hundreds of them, flying in silent circles high above the two sinister villains. They must have been nesting nearby to have arrived so quickly, and they must have been very thoroughly trained to be so eerily silent. Some of them looked very old, old enough to have been in the skies when the Baudelaire parents were children themselves. Some of them looked quite young, as if they had only recently emerged from the egg and were already obeying the shrill sound of a whistle. But all of them looked exhausted, as if they would rather be anywhere else but the summit of the Mortmain Mountains, doing absolutely anything rather than following the orders of such wretched people.

"Look at these creatures!" cried the woman with hair but no beard. "When the schism occurred, you may have won the carrier crows, volunteers, and you may have won the trained reptiles."

"Not anymore," Count Olaf said. "All of the reptiles except one—"

"Don't interrupt," the sinister woman interrupted. "You may have the carrier crows, but we have the two most powerful mammals in the world to do our bidding—the lions and eagles!"

"Eagles aren't *mammals*," Klaus cried out in frustration. "They're *birds*!"

"They're *slaves*," said the man with a beard but no hair, and the two villains reached into the pockets of their suits and drew out two long, wicked-looking whips. Violet and Klaus could see at once that they were similar to the whip

Olaf had used when bossing around the lions at Caligari Carnival. With matching, sinister sneers, the two mysterious villains cracked their whips in the air, and four eagles swooped down from the sky, landing on the strange thick pads that the villains had on their shoulders.

"These beasts will do anything we tell them to do," the woman said. "And today they're going to help us with our greatest triumph." She uncurled the whip and gestured to the ground around her, and the children noticed for the first time an enormous net on the ground, spread out over almost the entire peak and just stopping at their fork-assisted climbing shoes. "On my signal, these eagles will lift this net from the ground and carry it into the sky, capturing a group of young people who think they're here to celebrate False Spring."

"The Snow Scouts," Violet said in astonishment.

"We'll capture every one of those uniformed

brats," the villainous man bragged, "and each one of them will be offered the exciting opportunity to join us."

"They'll never join you," Klaus said.

"Of course they will," said the sinister woman, in her deep, deep voice. "They'll either be recruited, or they'll be our prisoners. But one thing is for certain—we'll burn down every single one of their parents' homes."

The two Baudelaires shuddered, and even Count Olaf looked a bit uneasy. "Of course," he said quickly, "the main reason we're doing all this is to get our hands on all those fortunes."

"Of course," Esmé said with a nervous snicker. "We'll have the Spats fortune, the Kornbluth fortune, the Winnipeg fortune, and many others. I'll be able to afford the penthouse apartment of every single building that isn't on fire!"

"Once you tell us where the sugar bowl is," said the man with a beard but no hair, "you can leave, volunteers, and take your baby friend with you. But wouldn't you rather join us?"

"No, thank you," Quigley said. "We're not interested."

"It doesn't matter if you're interested or not," said the woman with hair but no beard. "Look around you. You're hopelessly outnumbered. Wherever we go, we find new comrades who are eager to assist us in our work."

"We have comrades, too," Violet said bravely. "As soon as we rescue Sunny, we're going to meet up with the other volunteers at the last safe place, and tell them about your terrible scheme!"

"It's too late for that, volunteers," said Count Olaf in triumph. "Here come my new recruits!"

With a horrible laugh, the villain pointed in the direction of the rocky path, and the elder Baudelaires could see, past the covered casserole dish still held by the white-faced women, the arrival of the uniformed Snow Scouts, walking in two neat lines, more like eggs in a carton than young people on a hike. Apparently, the scouts had realized that the snow gnats were absent from this part of the Mortmain Mountains and had removed their masks, so Violet and Klaus could instantly spot Carmelita Spats, standing at the front of one of the lines with a tiara on her head—"tiara" is a word which here means "small crown given to a nasty little girl for no good reason"—and a large smirk on her face. Beside her, at the head of the other line, stood Bruce, holding the Springpole in one hand and a big cigar in the other. There was something about his face that Violet and Klaus found familiar, but they were too concerned about the villainous recruitment plan to give it much thought.

"What are all you cakesniffers doing here?" demanded Carmelita, in an obnoxious voice the two siblings found equally familiar. "I'm the False Spring Queen, and I order you to go away!"

"Now, now, Carmelita," Bruce said. "I'm sure these people are here to help celebrate your special day. Let's try to be accommodating. In fact, we should try to be accommodating, basic, calm, darling—"

The scouts had begun to say the ridiculous pledge along with Bruce, but the two Baudelaires knew they could not wait for the entire alphabetical list to be recited. "Bruce," Violet interrupted quickly, "these people are not here to help you celebrate False Spring. They're here to kidnap all of the Snow Scouts."

"What?" Bruce asked with a smile, as if the eldest Baudelaire might have been joking.

"It's a trap," Klaus said. "Please, turn around and lead the scouts away from here."

"Pay no attention to these three masked idiots," Count Olaf said quickly. "The mountain air has gone to their heads. Just take a few steps closer and we'll all join in a special celebration."

"We're happy to accommodate," Bruce said.

"After all, we're accommodating, basic—"

"No!" Violet cried. "Don't you see the net on the ground? Don't you see the eagles in the sky?"

"The net is decoration," Esmé said, with a smile as false as the Spring, "and the eagles are wildlife."

"Please listen to us!" Klaus said. "You're in terrible danger!"

Carmelita glared at the two Baudelaires, and adjusted her tiara. "Why should I listen to cakesniffing strangers like you?" she asked. "You're so stupid that you've still got your masks on, even though there aren't any snow gnats around here."

Violet and Klaus looked at one another through their masks. Carmelita's response had been quite rude, but the two siblings had to admit she had a point. The Baudelaires were unlikely to convince anyone that they were telling the truth while their faces were unnecessarily covered. They did not want to sacrifice their disguises and reveal their true identities to Count Olaf and his troupe, but they couldn't risk the kidnapping of all the Snow Scouts, even to save their sister. The two Baudelaires nodded at one another, and then turned to see that Quigley was nodding, too, and the three children reached up and took off their masks for the greater good.

Count Olaf's mouth dropped open in surprise. "You're dead!" he said to the eldest Baudelaire, saying something that he knew full well was ridiculous. "You perished in the caravan, along with Klaus!"

Esmé stared at Klaus, looking just as astonished as her boyfriend. "You're dead, too!" she cried. "You fell off a mountain!"

"And you're one of those twins!" Olaf said to Quigley. "You died a long time ago!"

"I'm not a twin," Quigley said, "and I'm not dead."

"And," Count Olaf said with a sneer, "you're not a volunteer. None of you are members of

V.F.D. You're just a bunch of orphan brats."

"In that case," said the woman with hair but no beard, in her deep, deep voice, "there's no reason to worry about that stupid baby any longer."

"That's true," Olaf said, and turned to the white-faced women. "Throw the baby off the mountain!" he ordered.

Violet and Klaus cried out in horror, but the two white-faced women merely looked at the covered casserole dish they were holding, and then at one another. Then, slowly, they looked at Count Olaf, but neither of them moved an inch.

"Didn't you hear me?" Olaf asked. "Throw that baby off this mountain!"

"No," said one of the white-faced women, and the two Baudelaires turned to them in relief.

"*No?*" asked Esmé Squalor in an astonished voice. "What do you mean, *no?*"

"We mean no," said the white-faced woman,

and her companion nodded. Together they put the covered casserole dish down on the ground in front of them. Violet and Klaus were surprised to see that the dish did not move, and assumed that their sister must have been too scared to come out.

"We don't want to participate in your schemes anymore," said the other white-faced woman, and sighed. "For a while, it was fun to fight fire with fire, but we've seen enough flames and smoke to last our whole lives."

"We don't think that it was a coincidence that our home burned to the ground," said the first woman. "We lost a sibling in that fire, Olaf."

Count Olaf pointed at the two women with a long, bony finger. "Obey my orders this *instant*!" he screamed, but his two former accomplices merely shook their heads, turned away from the villain, and began to walk away. Everyone on the square peak watched in silence as the two white-faced women walked past Count Olaf, past Esmé Squalor, past the two sinister villains with eagles on their shoulders, past the two Baudelaires and Quigley Quagmire, past the hook-handed man and the former employees of the carnival, and finally past Bruce and Carmelita Spats and the rest of the Snow Scouts, until they reached the rocky path and began to walk away from Mount Fraught altogether.

Count Olaf opened his mouth and let out a terrible roar, and jumped up and down on the net. "You can't walk away from me, you pasty-faced women!" he cried. "I'll find you and destroy you myself! In fact, I can do anything myself! I'm an individual practitioner, and I don't need anybody's help to throw this baby off the mountain!" With a nasty chuckle, he picked up the covered casserole dish, staggering slightly, and walked to the edge of the half-frozen waterfall.

"*No!*" Violet cried.

"*Sunny!*" Klaus screamed.

"Say good-bye to your baby sister, Baudelaires!" Count Olaf said, with a triumphant smile that showed all of his filthy teeth.

"I'm not a baby!" cried a familiar voice from under the villain's long, black automobile, and the two elder Baudelaires watched with pride and relief as Sunny emerged from behind the tire Violet had punctured, and ran to hug her siblings. Klaus had to take his glasses off to wipe the tears from his eyes as he was finally reunited with the young girl who was his sister. "I'm not a baby!" Sunny said again, turning to Olaf in triumph.

"How could this be?" Count Olaf said, but when he removed the cover from the casserole dish, he saw how this could be, because the object inside, which was about the same size and weight as the youngest Baudelaire, wasn't a baby either.

"Babganoush!" Sunny cried, which meant something along the lines of, "I concocted an escape plan with the eggplant that turned out to be even handier than I thought," but there was no need for anyone to translate, as the large vegetable slid out of the casserole dish and landed with a *plop!* at Olaf's feet.

"Nothing is going right for me today!" cried the villain. "I'm beginning to think that washing my face was a complete waste of time!"

"Don't upset yourself, boss," said Colette, contorting herself in concern. "I'm sure that Sunny will cook us something delicious with the eggplant."

"That's true," the hook-handed man said. "She's becoming quite a cook. The False Spring Rolls were quite tasty, and the lox was delicious."

"It could have used a little dill, in my opinion," Hugo said, but the three reunited Baudelaires turned away from this ridiculous conversation to face the Snow Scouts.

"Now do you believe us?" Violet asked Bruce. "Can't you see that this man is a terrible villain who is trying to do you harm?"

"Don't you remember us?" Klaus asked Carmelita Spats. "Count Olaf had a terrible scheme at Prufrock Prep, and he has a terrible scheme now!"

"Of course I remember you," Carmelita said. "You're those cakesniffing orphans who caused Vice Principal Nero all that trouble. And now you're trying to ruin my very special day! Give me that Springpole, Uncle Bruce!"

"Now, now, Carmelita," Bruce said, but Carmelita had already grabbed the long pole from Bruce's hands and was marching across the net toward the source of the Stricken Stream. The man with a beard but no hair and the woman with hair but no beard clasped their wicked whips and raised their shiny whistles to their sinister mouths, but the Baudelaires could see they were waiting to spring their trap until the rest of the scouts stepped forward, so they would be inside the net when the eagles lifted it from the ground.

"I crown myself False Spring Queen!" Carmelita announced, when she reached the very edge of Mount Fraught. With a nasty laugh of triumph, she elbowed the Baudelaires aside and drove the Springpole into the half-frozen top of the waterfall. There was a slow, loud shattering sound, and the Baudelaires looked down the slope and saw that an enormous crack was slowly making its way down the center of the waterfall, toward the pool and the two tributaries of the Stricken Stream. The Baudelaires gasped in horror. Although it was only the ice that was cracking, it looked as if the mountain were beginning to split in half, and that soon an enormous schism would divide the entire world.

"What are you looking at?" Carmelita asked scornfully. "Everybody's supposed to be doing a dance in my honor."

"That's right," Count Olaf said, "why doesn't everybody step forward and do a dance in honor of this darling little girl?"

"Sounds good to me," Kevin said, leading his fellow employees onto the net. "After all, I have two equally strong feet."

"And we should try to be accommodating," the hook-handed man said. "Isn't that what you said, Uncle Bruce?"

"Absolutely," Bruce agreed, with a puff on his cigar. He looked a bit relieved that all the arguing had ceased, and that the scouts finally had an opportunity to do the same thing they did every year. "Come on, Snow Scouts, let's recite the Snow Scout Alphabet Pledge as we dance around the Springpole."

The scouts cheered and followed Bruce onto the net. "Snow Scouts," the Snow Scouts said, "are accommodating, basic, calm, darling, emblematic, frisky, grinning, human, innocent, jumping, kept, limited, meek, nap-loving, official, pretty, quarantined, recent, scheduled, tidy, understandable, victorious, wholesome, xylophone, young, and zippered, every morning, every afternoon, every night, and all day long!"

There is nothing wrong, of course, with having a pledge, and putting into words what you might feel is important in your life as a reminder to yourself as you make your way in the world. If you feel, for instance, that well-read people are less likely to be evil, and a world full of people sitting quietly with good books in their hands is preferable to a world filled with schisms and sirens and other noisy and troublesome things, then every time you enter a library you might say to yourself, "The world is quiet here," as a sort of pledge proclaiming reading to be the greater good. If you feel that well-read people ought to be lit on fire and their fortunes stolen, you might adopt the saying "Fight fire with fire!" as your pledge, whenever you ordered one of your comrades around. But whatever words you might choose to describe your own life, there are two basic guidelines for composing a good pledge. One guideline is that the pledge make good sense, so that if your pledge contains the word "xylophone," for example, you mean that a percussion instrument played with mallets is very important to you, and not that you simply couldn't think of a good word that begins with the letter X. The other guideline is that the pledge be relatively short, so if a group of villains is luring you into a trap with a net and a group of exhausted trained eagles, you'll have more time to escape.

The Snow Scout Alphabet Pledge, sadly, did not follow either of these guidelines. As the Snow Scouts promised to be "xylophone," the man with a beard but no hair cracked his whip in the air, and the eagles sitting on both villains' shoulders began to flap their wings and, digging their claws into the thick pads, lifted the two sinister people high in the air, and when the pledge neared its end, and the Snow Scouts were all taking a big breath to make the snowy sound, the woman with hair but no beard blew her whistle, making a loud shriek the Baudelaires remembered from running laps as part of Olaf's scheme at Prufrock Prep. The three siblings stood with Quigley and watched as the rest of the eagles quickly dove to the ground, picked up the net, and, their wings trembling with the effort, lifted everyone who was standing on it into the air, the way you might remove all the dinner dishes from the table by lifting all the corners of the tablecloth. If you were to try such an unusual method of clearing the table, you would likely be sent to your room or chased out of the restaurant, and the results on Mount Fraught were equally disastrous. In moments, all of the Snow Scouts and Olaf's henchfolk were in an aerial heap, struggling together inside the net that the eagles were holding. The only person who escaped recruitment—besides the Baudelaires and Quigley Quagmire, of course—was Carmelita Spats, standing next to Count Olaf and his girlfriend.

"What's going on?" Bruce asked Count Olaf from inside the net. "What have you done?"

"I've triumphed," Count Olaf said, "*again*. A long time ago, I tricked you out of a reptile collection that I needed for my own use." The Baudelaires looked at one another in astonishment, suddenly realizing when they had met Bruce before. "And now, I've tricked you out of a collection of children!"

"What's going to happen to us?" asked one of the Snow Scouts fearfully.

"I don't care," said another Snow Scout, who seemed to be afflicted with Stockholm Syndrome already. "Every year we hike up to Mount Fraught and do the same thing. At least this year is a little different!"

"Why are you recruiting me, too?" asked the hook-handed man, and the Baudelaires could see one of his hooks frantically sticking out of the net. "I already work for you."

"Don't worry, hooky," Esmé replied mockingly. "It's all for the greater good!"

"Mush!" cried the man with a beard but no hair, cracking his whip in the air. Squawking in fear, the eagles began to drag the net across the sky, away from Mount Fraught.

"You get the sugar bowl from those bratty orphans, Olaf," ordered the woman with hair but no beard, "and we'll all meet up at the last safe place!"

"With these eagles at our disposal," the sinister man said in his hoarse voice, "we can finally catch up to that self-sustaining hot air mobile home and destroy those volunteers!"

The Baudelaires gasped, and shared an astonished look with Quigley. The villain was surely talking about the device that Hector had built at the Village of Fowl Devotees, in which Duncan and Isadora had escaped.

"We'll fight fire with fire!" the woman with hair but no beard cried in triumph, and the eagles carried her away. Count Olaf muttered something to himself and then turned and began creeping toward the Baudelaires. "I only need one of you to learn where the sugar bowl is," he said, his eyes shining brightly, "and to get my hands on the fortune. But which one should it be?"

"That's a difficult decision," Esmé said. "On one hand, it's been enjoyable having an infant servant. But it would be a lot of fun to smash Klaus's glasses and watch him bump into things."

"But Violet has the longest hair," Carmelita volunteered, as the Baudelaires backed toward the cracked waterfall with Quigley right behind them. "You could yank on it all the time, and tie it to things when you were bored."

"Those are both excellent ideas," Count Olaf said. "I'd forgotten what an adorable little girl you are. Why don't you join us?"

"Join you?" Carmelita asked.

"Look at my stylish dress," Esmé said to Carmelita. "If you joined us, I'd buy you all sorts of in outfits."

Carmelita looked thoughtful, gazing first at the children, and then at the two villains standing next to her and smiling. The three Baudelaires shared a look of horrified disappointment with Quigley. The siblings remembered how monstrous Carmelita had been at school, but it had never occurred to them that she would be interested in joining up with even more monstrous people.

"Don't believe them, Carmelita," Quigley said, and took his purple notebook out of his pocket. "They'll burn your parents' house down.

I have the evidence right here, in my common-place book."

"What are you going to believe, Carmelita?" Count Olaf asked. "A silly book, or something an adult tells you?"

"Look at us, you adorable little girl," Esmé said, her yellow, orange, and red dress crackling on the ground. "Do we look like the sort of people who like to burn down houses?"

"Carmelita!" Violet cried. "Don't listen to them!"

"Carmelita!" Klaus cried. "Don't join them!"

"Carmelita!" Sunny cried, which meant something like, "You're making a monstrous decision!"

"Carmelita," Count Olaf said, in a sickeningly sweet voice. "Why don't you choose one orphan to live, and push the others off the cliff, and then we'll all go to a nice hotel together."

"You'll be like the daughter we never had," Esmé said, stroking her tiara.

"Or something," added Olaf, who looked

like he would prefer having another employee rather than a daughter.

Carmelita glanced once more at the Baudelaires, and then smiled up at the two villains. "Do you really think I'm adorable?" she asked.

"I think you're adorable, beautiful, cute, dainty, eye-pleasing, flawless, gorgeous, harmonious, impeccable, jaw-droppingly adorable, keen, luscious, magnificent, nifty, obviously adorable, photogenic, quite adorable, ravishing, splendid, thin, undeformed, very adorable, well-proportioned, xylophone, yummy, and zestfully adorable," Esmé pledged, "every morning, every afternoon, every night, and all day long!"

"Don't listen to her!" Quigley pleaded. "A person can't be 'xylophone'!"

"I don't care!" Carmelita said. "I'm going to push these cakesniffers off the mountain, and start an exciting and fashionable new life!"

The Baudelaires took another step back,

and Quigley followed, giving the children a panicked look. Above them they could hear the squawking of the eagles as they took the villains' new recruits farther and farther away. Behind them they could feel the four drafts of the valley below, where the headquarters had been destroyed by people the children's parents had devoted their lives to stopping. Violet reached in her pocket for her ribbon, trying to imagine what she could invent that could get them away from such villainous people, and journeying toward their fellow volunteers at the last safe place. Her fingers brushed against the bread knife, and she wondered if she should remove the weapon from her pocket and use it to threaten the villains with violence, or whether this, too, would make her as villainous as the man who was staring at her now.

"Poor Baudelaires," Count Olaf said mockingly. "You might as well give up. You're hopelessly outnumbered."

"We're not outnumbered at all," Klaus said. "There are four of us, and only three of you."

"I count triple because I'm the False Spring Queen," Carmelita said, "so you *are* outnumbered, cakesniffers."

This, of course, was more utter nonsense from the mouth of this cruel girl, but even if it weren't nonsense, it does not always matter if one is outnumbered or not. When Violet and Klaus were hiking toward the Valley of Four Drafts, for instance, they were outnumbered by the swarm of snow gnats, but they managed to find Quigley Quagmire, climb up the Vertical Flame Diversion to the headquarters, and find the message hidden in the refrigerator. Sunny had been outnumbered by all of the villains on top of Mount Fraught, and had still managed to survive the experience, discover the location of the last safe place, and concoct a few recipes that were as easy as they were delicious. And the members of V.F.D. have always been outnumbered, because the number of greedy and wicked people always seems to be increasing, while more and more libraries go up in smoke, but the volunteers have managed to endure, a word which here means "meet in secret, communicate in code, and gather crucial evidence to foil the schemes of their enemies." It does not always matter whether there are more people on your side of the schism than there are on the opposite side, and as the Baudelaires stood with Quigley and took one more step back, they knew what was more important.

"Rosebud!" Sunny cried, which meant "In some situations, the location of a certain object can be much more important than being outnumbered," and it was true. As the villains gasped in astonishment, Violet sat down in the toboggan, grabbing the leather straps. Quigley sat down behind her and put his arms around her waist, and Klaus sat down next, and put his arms around Quigley's, and there was just enough room in back for a young girl, so Sunny sat behind her brother and hung on tight as

Violet pushed off from the peak of Mount Fraught and sent the four children hurtling down the slope. It did not matter that they were outnumbered. It only mattered that they could escape from a monstrous end by racing down the last of the slippery slope, just as it only matters for you to escape from a monstrous end by putting down the last of *The Slippery Slope*, and reading a book in which villains do not roar at children who are trying to escape.

"We'll be right behind you, Baudelaires!" Count Olaf roared, as the toboggan raced toward the Valley of Four Drafts, bumping and splashing against the cracked and melting ice.

"He won't be right behind us," Violet said. "My shoes punctured his tire, remember?"

Quigley nodded. "And he'll have to take that path," he said. "A car can't go down a waterfall."

"We'll have a head start," Violet said. "Maybe we can reach the last safe place before he does."

"Overhear!" Sunny cried. "Hotel Denouement!"

"Good work, Sunny!" Violet said proudly, pulling on the leather straps to steer the toboggan away from the large crack. "I knew you'd be a good spy."

"Hotel Denouement," Quigley said. "I think I have that in one of my maps. I'll check my commonplace book when we get to the bottom."

"Bruce!" Sunny cried.

"That's another thing to write down in our commonplace books," Klaus agreed. "That man Bruce was at Dr. Montgomery's house at the end of our stay. He said he was packing up Monty's reptile collection for the herpetological society."

"Do you think he's really a member of V.F.D.?" Violet asked.

"We can't be sure," Quigley said. "We've managed to investigate so many mysteries, and yet there's still so much we don't know." He sighed thoughtfully, and gazed down at the ruins of headquarters rushing toward them. "My siblings—"

But the Baudelaires never got to hear any more about Quigley's siblings, because at that moment the toboggan, despite Violet's efforts with the leather straps, slipped against a melted section of the waterfall, and the large sled began to spin. The children screamed, and Violet grabbed the straps as hard as she could, only to have them break in her hands. "The steering mechanism is broken!" she yelled. "Dragging Esmé Squalor up the slope must have weakened the straps!"

"Uh-oh!" Sunny cried, which meant something along the lines of, "That doesn't sound like good news."

"At this velocity," Violet said, using a scientific word for speed, "the toboggan won't stop when we reach the frozen pool. If we don't slow down, we'll fall right into the pit we dug."

Klaus was getting dizzy from all the spinning, and closed his eyes behind his glasses. "What can we do?" he asked.

"Drag your shoes against the ice!" Violet cried. "The forks should slow us down!"

Quickly, the two elder Baudelaires stretched out their legs and dragged the forks of their shoes against the last of the ice on the slope. Quigley followed suit, but Sunny, who of course was not wearing fork-assisted climbing shoes, could do nothing but listen to the scraping and splashing of the forks against the thawing ice of the stream as the toboggan slowed ever so slightly.

"It's not enough!" Klaus cried. As the toboggan continued to spin, he caught brief glimpses of the pit they had dug, covered with a thin layer of weakened wood, getting closer and closer as the four children hurtled toward the bottom of the waterfall.

"Bicuspid?" Sunny asked, which meant something like "Should I drag my teeth against the ice, too?"

"It's worth a try," Klaus said, but as soon as the youngest Baudelaire leaned down and dragged her teeth along the thawing waterfall, the Baudelaires could see at once that it was not really worth a try at all, as the toboggan kept spinning and racing toward the bottom.

"That's not enough, either," Violet said, and focused her inventing mind as hard as she could, remembering how she had stopped the caravan, when she and her brother were hurtling away from Count Olaf's automobile. There was nothing large enough to use as a drag chute, and the eldest Baudelaire found herself wishing that Esmé Squalor were on board with them, so she could stop the toboggan with her enormous, flame-imitating dress. She knew there was no blackstrap molasses, wild clover honey, corn syrup, aged balsamic vinegar, apple butter, strawberry jam, caramel sauce, maple syrup, butterscotch topping, maraschino liqueur, virgin and extra-virgin olive oil, lemon curd, dried apricots, mango chutney, *crema di noci*, tamarind paste, hot mustard, marshmallows, creamed corn, peanut butter, grape preserves, salt water taffy, condensed milk, pumpkin pie filling, or glue on board, or any other sticky substance, for that matter. But then she remembered the small table she had used to drag on the ground, behind the caravan, and she reached into her pocket and knew what she could do.

"Hang on!" Violet cried, but she did not hang on herself. Dropping the broken straps of the toboggan, she grabbed the long bread knife and took it out of her pocket at last. It had only been several days, but it felt like a very long time since she had taken the knife from the caravan, and it seemed that every few minutes she had felt its jagged blade in her pocket as she tried to defeat the villains high above her, without becoming a villain herself. But now, at last, there was something she could do with the knife that might save them all, without hurting anyone. Gritting her teeth, Violet leaned out of the spinning toboggan and thrust the knife as hard as she could into the ice of the slippery slope.

The tip of the blade hit the crack caused by

Carmelita's Springpole, and then the entire knife sank into the slope just as the toboggan reached the bottom. There was a sound the likes of which the Baudelaires had never heard, like a combination of an enormous window shattering and the deep, booming sound of someone firing a cannon. The knife had widened the crack, and in one tremendous crash, the last of the ice fell to pieces and all of the forks, sunlight, teeth, and tobogganing finally took their toll on the waterfall. In one enormous *whoosh!*, the waters of the Stricken Stream came rushing down the slope, and in a moment the Baudelaires were no longer on a frozen pool at the bottom of a strange curve of ice, but simply at the bottom of a rushing waterfall, with gallons and gallons of water pouring down on them. The orphans had just enough time to take a deep breath before the toboggan was forced underwater. The three siblings hung on tight, but the eldest Baudelaire felt a pair of hands slip from her waist, and when the wooden toboggan bobbed to the surface again, she called out the name of her lost friend.

"*Quigley!*" she screamed.

"*Violet!*" The Baudelaires heard the triplet's voice as the toboggan began to float down one of the tributaries. Klaus pointed, and through the rush of the waterfall the children could see a glimpse of their friend. He had managed to grab onto a piece of wood from the ruins of headquarters, something that looked a bit like a banister, such as one might need to walk up a narrow staircase leading to an astronomical observatory. The rush of the water was dragging the wood, and Quigley, down the opposite tributary of the Stricken Stream.

"*Quigley!*" Violet screamed again.

"*Violet!*" Quigley shouted, over the roar of the water. The siblings could see he had removed his commonplace book from his pocket and was desperately waving it at them. "*Wait for me! Wait for me at—*"

But the Baudelaires heard no more. The

Stricken Stream, in its sudden thaw from the arrival of False Spring, whisked the banister and the toboggan away from one another, down the two separate tributaries. The siblings had one last glimpse of the notebook's dark purple cover before Quigley rushed around one twist in the stream, and the Baudelaires rushed around another, and the triplet was gone from their sight.

"*Quigley!*" Violet called, one more time, and tears sprung in her eyes.

"He's alive," Klaus said, and held Violet's shoulder to help her balance on the bobbing toboggan. She could not tell if the middle Baudelaire was crying, too, or if his face was just wet from the waterfall. "He's alive, and that's the important thing."

"Intrepid," Sunny said, which meant something like, "Quigley Quagmire was brave and resourceful enough to survive the fire that destroyed his home, and I'm sure he'll survive this, too."

Violet could not bear that her friend was

rushing away from her, so soon after first making his acquaintance. "But we're supposed to wait for him," she said, "and we don't know where."

"Maybe he's going to try to reach his siblings before the eagles do," Klaus said, "but we don't know where they are."

"Hotel Denouement?" Sunny guessed. "V.F.D.?"

"Klaus," Violet said, "you saw some of Quigley's research. Do you know if these two tributaries ever meet up again?"

Klaus shook his head. "I don't know," he said. "Quigley's the cartographer."

"Godot," Sunny said, which meant "We don't know where to go, and we don't know how to get there."

"We know some things," Klaus said. "We know that someone sent a message to J.S."

"Jacques," Sunny said.

Klaus nodded. "And we know that the message said to meet on Thursday at the last safe place."

"Matahari," Sunny said, and Klaus smiled, and pulled Sunny toward him so she wouldn't fall off the floating toboggan. She was no longer a baby, but the youngest Baudelaire was still young enough to sit on her brother's lap.

"Yes," Klaus agreed. "Thanks to you, we know that the last safe place is the Hotel Denouement."

"But we don't know where that is," Violet said. "We don't know where to find these volunteers, or if indeed there are any more surviving members of V.F.D. We can't even be certain what V.F.D. stands for, or if our parents are truly dead. Quigley was right. We've managed to investigate so many mysteries, and yet there's still so much we don't know."

Her siblings nodded sadly, and if I had been there at that moment, instead of arriving far too late to see the Baudelaires, I would have nodded, too. Even for an author like myself, who has dedicated his entire life to investigating the mysteries that surround the Baudelaire case, there is still much I have been unable to discover. I do not know, for instance, what happened to the two white-faced women who decided to quit Olaf's troupe and walk away, all by themselves, down the Mortmain Mountains. There are some who say that they still paint their faces white, and can be seen singing sad songs in some of the gloomiest music halls in the city. There are some who say that they live together in the hinterlands, attempting to grow rhubarb in the dry and barren ground. And there are those who say that they did not survive the trip down from Mount Fraught, and that their bones can be found in one of the many caves in the odd, square peaks. But although I have sat through song after dreary song, and tasted some of the worst rhubarb in my life, and brought bone after bone to a skeleton expert until she told me that I was making her so miserable that I should never return, I have not been able to discover what truly happened to the two women. I do not know where the remains of the caravan are, as I have told you, and as I reach the end of the rhyming dictionary, and read the short list of words that rhyme with "zucchini," I am beginning to think I should stop my search for the destroyed vehicle and give up that particular part of my research. And I have not tracked down the refrigerator in which the Baudelaires found the Verbal Fridge Dialogue, despite stories that it is also in one of the Mortmain Mountain caves, or performing in some of the gloomiest music halls in the city.

But even though there is much I do not know, there are a few mysteries that I have solved for certain, and one thing I am sure about is where the Baudelaire orphans went next, as the ashen waters of the Stricken Stream hurried their toboggan out of the Mortmain Mountains, just as the sugar bowl was hurried along, after the volunteer tossed it into the stream to save it from the fire. But although I know exactly where the Baudelaires went, and can even trace their path on a map drawn by one of the most promising young cartographers of our time, I am not the writer who can describe it best. The writer who can most accurately and elegantly describe the path of the three orphans was an associate of mine who, like the man who wrote "The Road Less Traveled," is now dead. Before he died, however, he was widely regarded as a very good poet, although some people think his writings about religion were a little too mean-spirited. His name was Algernon Charles Swinburne, and the last quatrain of the eleventh stanza of his poem "The Garden of Proserpine" perfectly describes what the children found as this chapter in their story drew to an end, and the next one began. The first half of the quatrain reads,

> *That no life lives forever;*
> *That dead men rise up never;*

and indeed, the grown men in the Baudelaires' lives who were dead, such as Jacques Snicket, or the children's father, were never going to rise up. And the second half of the quatrain reads,

That even the weariest river
Winds somewhere safe to sea.

This part is a bit trickier, because some poems are a bit like secret codes, in that you must study them carefully in order to discover their meaning. A poet such as Quigley Quagmire's sister, Isadora, of course, would know at once what those two lines mean, but it took me quite some time before I decoded them. Eventually, however, it became clear that "the weariest river" refers to the Stricken Stream, which indeed seemed weary from carrying away all of the ashes from the destruction of V.F.D. headquarters, and that "winds somewhere safe to sea" refers to the last safe place where all the volunteers, including Quigley Quagmire, could gather. As Sunny said, she and her siblings did not know where to go, and they didn't know how to get there, but the Baudelaire orphans were winding there anyway, and that is one thing I know for certain.

Meredith Heuer © 2003

Until recently, **LEMONY SNICKET** was presumed to be "presumed dead." Instead, this "presumed" presumption wasn't disproved to not be incorrect. As he continues with his investigation, interest in the Baudelaire case has increased. So has his horror.

Visit him on the Web at www.lemonysnicket.com

BRETT HELQUIST
was born in Ganado, Arizona, grew up in Orem, Utah, and now lives in Brooklyn, New York. He earned a bachelor's degree in fine arts from Brigham Young University and has been illustrating ever since. His work deciphering the evidence provided by Lemony Snicket into pictures often leaves him so distraught that he is awake late into the night.

To My Kind Editor —

I apologize for the watery
quality of this letter, but I'm
afraid the ink I am using
has become diluted, a word
which here means "soaked
with salt water from the
ocean and from the author's
own tears." It is difficult
to conduct my investigation
on the damaged submarine
where the Baudelaires lived
during this episode of their
lives, and I can only hope
that the rest of this letter
will not wash away.

The Grim Gr